THE MAN WHO SHOT OUT MY EYE IS DEAD

STORIES

THE MAN WHO SHOT OUT MY EYE IS DEAD

STORIES

CHANELLE BENZ

An Imprint of HarperCollins*Publishers*

THE MAN WHO SHOT OUT MY EYE IS DEAD. Copyright © 2017 by Chanelle Benz. All rights reserved. Printed in the United States of America. No part of this book may be used or reproduced in any manner whatsoever without written permission except in the case of brief quotations embodied in critical articles and reviews. For information address HarperCollins Publishers, 195 Broadway, New York, NY 10007.

HarperCollins books may be purchased for educational, business, or sales promotional use. For information please e-mail the Special Markets Department at SPsales@harpercollins.com.

Ecco® and HarperCollins® are trademarks of HarperCollins Publishers.

FIRST EDITION

Library of Congress Cataloging-in-Publication Data has been applied for.

ISBN 978-0-06-249075-9

17 18 19 20 21   RRD   10 9 8 7 6 5 4 3 2 1

For Christine, Honora, & Violet Ashwell

CONTENTS

THE MAN WHO SHOT OUT MY EYE IS DEAD

STORIES

West of the Known

My brother was the first man to come for me. The first man I saw in the raw, profuse with liquor, outside a brothel in New Mexico Territory. He was the first I know to make a promise then follow on through. There is nothing to forgive. For in the high violence of joy, is there not often a desire to swear devotion? But what then? When is it ever brung off to the letter? When they come for our blood, we will not end, but go on in an unworldly fever.

I come here to collect, my brother said from the porch. If there was more I did not hear it for Uncle Bill and Aunt Josie stepped out and closed the door. I was in the kitchen canning tomatoes, standing over a row of mason jars, hands dripping a wa'try red when in stepped a man inside a long buckskin coat.

I'm your brother, Jackson, the man smiled, holding out his hand.

I did not know him. And he did not in particular look like me.

I'm Lavenia, I said, frantic to find an apron to wipe upon.

I know who you are, he said.

I put my hands up.

Dudn't matter, he said, and the red water dripped down his wrist, We're kin.

With the sun behind him, he stood in shadow. Like the white rider of the Four Horsemen come to conquest, and I would've cut my heart out for him then.

Jackson walked to the stove and handed me down an apron from a hook, saying, I reckon we got the same eye color. But your shape's your ma's.

I couldn't not go. Uncle Bill and Aunt Josie saw me fed but were never cherishing. I did not dread them as I did their son, Cy.

What comes in the dark?

Stars.

Cooler air.

Dogs' bark.

Cy.

Always I heard his step before the door and I knew when it was not the walking by kind. I would not move from the moment my cousin came in, till the moment he went out, from when he took down my nightdress, till I returned to myself to find how poorly the cream bow at my neck had been tied.

In the morning, when Cy was about to ride into town and I was feeding the chickens, we might joke and talk, or try. I had known Cy all my remembered life. We had that tapestry of family to draw upon.

The night Jackson came for me, I heard Cy's step. My carpetbag, which I had yet to fill, fell from my hands. Hush said the air, like a hand in the dark coming for your mouth. Cy came in and went to my bedroom window, fists in his pockets, watching the ox in the field knock about with its bell. Drunk. Not certain how, since no one at dinner had any spirits but Jackson, who'd brought his own bottle and tucked in like it was his last meal.

You gonna go with him, huhn? Cy spoke through his teeth, a miner having once broken his jaw.

He is my brother, I said.

Half-brother, Cy said, turning toward me.

He's older'n me so I guess I best listen, I said, suddenly dreadfully frightened that somehow they would not let me leave.

Jackson an me're the same age. Both born in '50. You remember when he lived here? It was you and Jackson and your ma.

I don't remember Ma and I don't remember Jackson, I said.

It were a real to-do: your pa joining up to be a Reb, leaving us his kids and squaw. She was a fine thing tho. That Indian gal. They lost you know . . . Cy sat me down on the bed by my wrist. . . . The Rebs. His hands pinching the tops of my arms, he laid me back. You know what kind of man Jackson is? I heard Cy ask. He was a damned horse thief. Old John Cochran only let him go cause of my pa.

You done? Jackson leaned in the doorway, whittling a stick into a stake.

I jumped up. I'm sorry I'm just getting started, I said, kneeling to pick up the carpetbag.

Get a wiggle on, girl, Jackson said, coming in.

Cy walked out, knocking Jackson's shoulder as he passed.

Jackson smiled. Hey now, I don't wanna put a spoke in your wheel, but how you think you're gonna load all that on one horse?

I'm sorry. Is it too much? I whispered and stopped.

Why are you whispering? he asked.

I don't want them to think we're in here doing sumthin bad, I said and lifted open the trunk at the bottom of my bed.

Look here, Jackson said, You're gonna come live with me and my best pal, Colt Wallace, in New Mexico Territory. And Sal Adams, if we can locate the bastard, so pack as little as you can.

Jackson made like he was gonna sit on the bed, but instead picked my bustle up off the quilt. I got no notion how you women wear these things, he said.

I don't need to bring that, I said.

You know, Lavenia, you weren't afraid of nuthin. When I was here you was a game little kid. He spun the bustle up and caught it.

I disremember, I said.

He looked at me, the tip of his knife on his bottom lip, then went back to whittling. When I'm with you, I won't let no one hurt you. You know that? he called back as he walked toward the kitchen.

—:—

Jackson threw me up on the horse, saying, Stay here till I come back. An don't get down for nuthin. Promise me.

Yessir. I promise, I said, shooing a mosquito from my neck, I swear on my mother's grave.

Don't do that, he said.

Why? I asked.

Cause she weren't a Christian.

Wait.

What?

Nuthin.

The dark of the Texas plain was a solid thing, surrounding, collecting on my face like blued dust. The plain and I waited in the stretched still till we heard the first gunshot, yes, then a lopsided shouting fell out the back of the house. The chickens disbanded. A general caterwauling collapsed into one dragged weeping that leaked off into the dogs the stars and the cool.

Jackson opened the door and the horse shifted under me.

Please, I asked, What did you do?

Jackson tossed the bloody stake into the scrub and holstered his pistol. I killed that white-livered son of a bitch, he said, jerking my horse alongside his.

And the others? I asked.

You know they knew, don't ya? Aunt Josie and Uncle Bill. He let go and pulled up ahead, They knew about Cy. Now you know sumthin, too, he said.

Through the dark I followed him.

—:—

A few mornings after, we rode into a town consisting of a general store, two saloons, and a livery. We harnessed the horses round the back of one of the saloons. Jackson dug a key out from under a barrel and we took the side door. He went behind the empty bar and set down two scratched glasses.

You used to be more chipper, he said. Don't be sore. An eye for an eye is in the Bible.

There's a lot of things in the Bible. Thou shalt not kill, for one, I said, sitting up on a stool.

Waal, the Bible is a complicated creature, he said, smiling.

And you and I're living in Old Testament times. He poured me a double rye. I can't warn a trespasser with no sugar tongue. I have to make it so he don't come back and you don't go bout that cordially, minding your manners. No ma'am, I have to avenge the harm done upon me. But I can tell you that I don't kill wantonly.

And I don't drink liquor, I said, pushing the glass back across the wood still wet from the night.

Truth is, he clinked my glass, I shouldn't have left you. When I run away I mean. It's jest being you was a girl, and so little, a baby almost, I figured Bill an Josie'd take to you like you was their own, especially after your ma and our pa went and died. But those folks didn't do right. They didn't do right at all. We can agree on that, can't we?

I don't know I guess we can, I said and a rat run under my feet.

Those folks, they weren't expecting me to come back. But no one's gonna hurt you when I'm around—that there is a promise.

I picked up my glass. We'd run out of food on the trail the morning before and as we broke camp, Jackson'd made me a cigarette for breakfast.

But I didn't know what you were fixing to do, I said, running my tongue over the taste of ash in my mouth.

You didn't? Let me look about me for that Bible cause I'd like you to swear on it.

Can you even read?

Enough. Cain't spell tho. He refilled my glass, Look, it ain't your fault this world is no place for women.

But us women are in it, I said.

Have another, he said. Don't dwell.

A bare-armed woman appeared in a ribboned shift, breasts

henned up; she went into Jackson and said Spanish things. He smiled, giving her a squeeze, Go on then, he said to me. Go with Rosa, she'll take care a you. Imma go get a shave and a haircut. Should I get my mustache waxed and curled?

I laughed despite myself. The whore held out her hand, Come with me, Labinya.

Upstairs, she poured water in a washstand. Some slipped over the side and spilled onto the floor; she smiled then helped me take off my clothes heavy with stain. Her nose had been broken and she was missing two top teeth on either side. I stood there while the whore washed me like a baby. I wondered if this was something she did to men, lingering on their leafless parts for money.

On the bed, divested, I could not care what next would befall me. There was no sheet only a blanket; I covered my head with the itch of it and cried. I cried cause as sure as Hell was hot I was glad Cy was gone, cause I could not understand why when first Jackson took my hand I had known he was not good but bad, and I knew that right then I was good but would be bad in the days to come, which were forever early and there as soon as you closed your eyes.

The whore was still in the room. But when I grew quiet, the door shut, and I could not hear her step, for the whore was not wearing shoes.

—:—

Since I was between hay and grass, my brother dressed me as a boy. It only needed a bandanna. I's tall for my age and all long lines so it was my lack of Adam's apple he had to hide if I was gonna work with him and not for the cathouse, since my face was comely enough tho never pleased him, it looking too much like my mother's (he said and I did not know).

In the back of the saloon, the bandanna Jackson was tying bit the hair at the nape of my neck. Lord, I think you grew an inch these last few months, Jackson said then turned my chin to him. Why're you making that face?

Cause it pulls, I said, playing with my scabbard. Jackson had gotten me a whole outfit: a six-shooter, belt and cartridges.

Waal, why didn't you say so? Needs to be shorter, he whipped the bandanna off, Hey Rosa, gimme them scissors again. What d'ya mean no por favor? She said you got pretty hair, Lav. Rosa, why don't you make yourself useful and get us some coffee from the hotel—Arbuckle if they got it—and have that barkeep pour me another whiskey on your way out. Lavenia, I am gonna cut it all off if that is all right with you.

I shrugged as Colt Wallace of the white-blond hair who could speak Dutch and play the fiddle came into the saloon with Sal Adams who always wore a big black hat and had told me when he taught me three-card monte that his father had one lung and ate only turnips.

Hey boys, you ready for a hog-killing time tomorrow? Sit down here, honey. See Rosa, Lavenia don't mind! Jackson shouted to the whore who was going out into the night and across the street in her trinkets and paint.

Jackson, said Colt, dragging a chair to our table away from the games of chance. What are you doing to the fair Lavenia Bell?

Keeping her from launching into a life of shame, an helping her into one of profit, Jackson said, and my black hair fell down around me. Sal, gimme her hat. Lavenia, stand up. Go on. There. She looks more like a boy now, don't she?

Sal smiled and said, A boy with a woman's heart.

Colt gave an old-fashioned Comanche yell, then said, Sure she looks like a boy cause she's flat as an ironing—

Jackson had both hands round Colt's throat. The table tipped and Sal stepped in the middle of them, steadying it. Fall back, Jackson, Sal said. Colt misspoke. Didn't you? You understand, Colt, how such words might offend?

Choking, Colt tried to nod.

Please don't, Jackson! I ain't hurt none by it. Truly, I said. Listen, I don't even want breasts.

Why not? Jackson turned to look at me.

I don't know—guess they'd get in the way of shootin?

Jackson laughed and let him loose.

Sure Sal, coughed Colt. I mean, I didn't mean nothing by it, Jackie. I meant to say they'll think Lav's a boy long as they don't look at her in the eyes.

What the hell you mean by that? Jackson asked, rounding on Colt again.

He means she's got long eyelashes, Sal said, taking our drinks from one of the whores.

Shoot Jackie, ain't we friends? Here, Colt toasted, To good whiskey and bad women!

—◂:▸—

It was a day's ride. Sal stayed to guard the town square and watch for any vigilant citizens with guns, while Colt and I went with Jackson into the bank, the heft of worry in my bowels. There was only one customer inside, a round man in spectacles, who Colt thrust into and said, Hands up, with his loud flush of a laugh, as Jackson and I slid over the counter, six-shooters out, shouting for the two bank tellers to get down on their knees.

Open up that vault, said Jackson.

We can't do that, sir, the older teller said. Only the bank manager has the key. And he's not here today.

Get the goddamn money. This whole town knows you got a key.

Sir, I would if I could but—

You think I got time for this? Jackson hammered the older teller in the face with his pistol, and the man thrashed over, cupping his nose. Jackson straddled him as he lay on the ground, saying, Now you open that vault right quick.

The older teller blinked up at him through bloody hands, I won't do that. I refuse to be . . .

Jackson thumped the older teller's head with the butt of his right pistol and that older teller began to leak his brain. There was a sting in my nose as I watched him drip into the carpet. Until then, I had no notion that blood was child-book red. Jackson turned to the younger teller, who looked frantic at me.

Son, you wanna live? Jackson asked.

I willed him to nod.

Gesturing to me, Jackson said, Give this boy here all the bonds, paper currency and coin in these bags.

Hurry it up back there! hollered Colt, forcing the customer to his knees and peeking out the front door, Sumthin's up! Sal's bringin the horses!

Me and the younger teller, Jackson's pistol cocked on him, stuffed the burlap sacks as Jackson climbed backward through the bank window. That's enough. Now get on your knees, he said.

As I tossed Jackson the first sack, the young teller rose up and grabbed me from behind, snatching my gun, waving it

at us, shouting, You cowardly bushwackers, attacking an un-
armed man! You're a whore herder—this girl is a girl!

Jackson shot the young teller in the chest, dove through the
window and got back my gun. He slapped it into my stomach.
Shoot him, he said.

Who? No, I pushed the gun away.

Hey! Colt shouted, What in hell is goin on? They're gonna
have heard them shots!

I looked to the young teller rearing in his blood. Please
Jackson, don't make me do that, I said.

Put him out of his misery, honey. He's gonna die either way.

I raised the gun then just as quick lowered it. I cain't, I said.

You're with us, ain't ya? Jackson was standing behind me,
the warm of his hand went on the meat of my back, After all
Lavenia, you just done told that boy my name.

Colt's gun sounded twice from the front.

And so I shot the young teller dead through the eye and out
of that bank we rode into the bright forever.

—:—

Alone, jest us two, in what I had by then guessed was her actual
room, tho it had none of the marks of the individual, the whore
put the whiskey between my fingers.

Èl no debería haber hecho esto, she said, locking the door
and loosening my bandanna.

Leave it, I stared in her mirror. Make me drunk, I said. I
want the bitter of that oh-be-joyful.

Drink. She put the glass to my lips, then took it back and
topped it off, asking, How old you?

Fifteen. Sixteen in June, I said. The whiskey tore a line down my stomach to let the hot in. Wait. If you can speak English, then why don't you?

She shrugged, handing me back a full glass, Is more easy for men to think the other.

And I ain't a man, I said.

She nodded. Why you brother dress you like one?

So when we ride no man messes with me and I don't mess with my bustle. Is it hard being a—a soiled dove? I drank. It's awful hard on one being a gunslinger.

She smiled with her missing teeth, took off my coat and shirt then sat down inside the bell of her ruffled skirt. My husband die when I you age, she said. I make good money this place.

Money . . . I repeated, and took the whiskey off her bureau where it sat next to a knife and a small bottle of Best Turkey Laudanum. I got money now I guess, I said and laid a few dollars down. If you don't mind, I said and droppered laudanum into my whiskey, I hope this will stupefy me. I drank it and flopped back on the bed.

Where you mama?

Dead. When I was three. My pa's sister raised me. Aunt Josie.

You papa?

I shook my head, Dead from the war.

Solo Jackson, she said.

Hey Rosa, what if sumthin bad happened that I did?

The door handle turned, then came a knocking and my brother: Hey Rosa, lemme in there. I gotta see her. Lavenia?

I scrambled up.

Rosa put her finger to her lips, Lavenia no here.

She's gotta be—hey, Lavenia, Lavenia! C'mon now. Come out and jest let me talk to ya for a minute, honey.

I swallowed more whiskey'd laudanum. Hey Rosa, I whispered, holding out my free hand.

No now, Jackie, Rosa said, taking it.

If you did a bad thing but you didn't mean to? Cause he was gonna die anyways either way. I pulled till her head went under my chin. But he was alive and then he wasn't and I did that, I did.

Jackson no good.

No, no good, I said.

You have money? You take and go. Far.

But I'm no good, I said.

Open this damn door! Jackson pounded. Listen Rosa, your pussy ain't worth so much to me that I won't beat your face off.

Hush up! I shouted, Shut your mouth! The shaking door stilled. I don't want you, I said.

Lavenia, I heard him slide down the door. Hey, don't be like that.

I leaned my forearm and head onto the wood. Why? I asked.

Baby girl, he said, don't be sore. Not at me. I cain't.

Why did you make me? I asked.

Darlin, those men seen our faces. What we did we had to do in order to save ourselves. That there was self-defense. Sure, it's a hard lesson, I ain't gonna falsify that to you.

But I'm wicked now, I said, feeling a wave of warm roll me over. I slid.

Hey, I heard him get to his feet, Hey you lemme in there.

Rosa put her hand over mine where it rested on the lock. The augury of her eyes was not lost on me. As soon as I opened the door, Jackson fell through, then tore after her.

Jackson don't, I yanked him by the elbow as he took her by the neck. You—she didn't do nothing but what I told her to!

He shook me off but let her go. Go on, get out, he slammed

the door and galloped me onto the bed, tackling me from behind and squeezing until I tear'd. I did not drift up and away but instead stayed there in what felt to be the only room for miles and miles around. He spoke into my hair, saying, We're in this together.

Jackson, I sniffed and kicked his shin with the back of my heel, Too tight.

He exhaled and went loose, The fellas are missing you down there.

No, they ain't.

They're saying they cain't celebrate without the belle of the Bell's.

I rolled to face him, pushing the stubble of his chin into my forehead, Why do you want to make me you?

Would you rather be a daughter of sin?

I *am* a daughter of sin.

You know what I mean. A . . . Jackson searched his mind, A frail sister.

I could not help but laugh. He whooped, ducking my punches till he wrestled me off the bed and I got a bloody nose. You hurt? he asked, leaning over the edge.

Lord, I don't know, I shrugged in a heap on the floor, sweet asleep but awake. I cain't feel a thing. Like it's afternoon in me, I said.

Jackson glanced over at the laudanum bottle and backhanded me sharp and distant. Don't you ever do that again, you hear?

My nose trickled doubly but I said, It doesn't hurt. I tried to peel Jackson's hands off his face, Hey it truly truly doesn't!

I laughed and he laughed and we went down to the saloon drinking spirits till we vomited our bellies and heads empty.

—:—

The next night two deputies walked into the saloon and shot out the lights. In the exchange of dark and flash, a set of hands yanked me down. I'd been drinking while Jackson was with Rosa upstairs. I got out my six-shooter but did not know how to pick a shadow. A man hissed near my head and I crawled with him to the side door.

Out of the fog of the saloon, Colt stood, catching his breath, saying, There ain't nothing we can do for Jackson and Sal. If they take them to the jail, we'll break them out. C'mon.

No, I said, getting up.

A couple bystanders that had been gawking at the saloon were now looking to us.

Lavenia, Colt took me tight by the shoulder, and swayed us like two drunkards into the opposite direction. In the candle-light of passing houses, Colt's hand, cut by glass, bled down my arm.

At the end of the alley, Colt turned us to where three horses were on a hitch-rack. We crouched, untying the reins, and tho my horse gave a snort, it did not object to the thievery, but we were not able to ride out of town unmolested. The sheriff and his deputy were waiting and threw us lead. Buckshot found my shoulder, and found Colt, too, who slid like spit down his horse and onto his back, dead.

—:—

Hey there Deputy, said Jackson through the bars, How much for a clean sheet of paper and that pen?

The men outside the jail began shouting louder. The silver-haired sheriff sat at his desk, writing up a report, ignoring us all.

This un? the deputy stopped his pacing.

I'll give you twenty whole dollars, Jackson said. I'll be real surprised if I make it to trial, so least you could do is honor my last request.

There were a few scattered thumps on the door.

Won't we make it to trial? I asked.

Well darlin, there's a mob out there that's real upset bout me shooting that bank teller and that marshal and that faro dealer and that one fella—what was he? A professor of the occult sciences!

I laughed. The men kicked at the door. The sheriff checked his Winchester.

Jackson chuckled, I'm writing against the clock. The windows smashed as if by a flock of birds. Jackson didn't look up from writing.

Now sheriff, you won't let them hurt my baby girl will ya? You gotta preach to them like you was at Judgment Day. Gotta tell them that this young girl here was jest following me, was under a powerful family sway. Deputy, would you kindly give this to her.

The deputy took the letter.

The sheriff said, Son, there are about forty men out there with the name of your gang boiling in their blood. By law the two of us must protect you and that child. I jest hope we don't die in the attempt.

Thee Dream—
    Dremp't I was with you, Lav,
    near yur breth so dear.

I never new no one lik you
and I wisht you wer near.
No Angel on earth or Heven,
could rival your Hart,
no Deth or distunce can Us part.
If any shud tell you
they love you eternully,
there is no one you tell em
who Loves you lik Me.

Fare well! My sister and frend,

Allso my Bell of Bells,

Yors I Hope,
Jackson Bell

The forty exited the street and entered our cells.

They dragged Jackson and I into the dogs the stars the cool and the night. Their hands in what hair I had; my hands underbrush-burned and bound together in bailing wire.

In an abandoned stable somewhere behind the jail, they made Jackson stand on a crate and put the noose hanging from the rafters round his neck. They were holding down the deputy and the sheriff, who looked eyeless cause of the blood, having been beaten over the head.

I was brought to Jackson and saw the rope round his neck weren't even clean.

Hey gal, my brother said, You're my final request. Now what do you think? Don't you think I kept my promise to you? You'll be all right. If you cain't find Sal, Rosa will take care a you.

I nodded and the men pulled me back.

Hey you ain't crying, are ya? Jackson called out, swallowing against the rope. C'mon, quick—you got any last thing to say to me?

The men brought me to a crate and tied a noose around my neck.

What the hell's going on? Jackson asked.

You all cannot murder a woman without a fair trial, the sheriff started up.

Now fellas, it ain't s'posed to go like this. Listen to the sheriff here— Jackson said and the men walloped him in the belly.

Lavenia Bell, the men asked, crowding me, What is your final request?

Sometimes I wish I were just a regular girl, not a whore or an outlaw or playacting a man. I had a father for two years and a mother for three, but I cannot remember what that was like, if they care for you better or hurt you less or if they keep you no matter what it costs them.

The girl first, the men said.

I am not afraid, I said. You kept your promise good. Thank you for you.

Have you no wives, no sisters or daughters? shouted the sheriff.

I felt the thick of hands on my waist.

Wait! Don't y'all see? She would never done nuthin without me not without me—

The noose tightened.

The sheriff was struggling to get to his feet, hollering. Boys this will weigh heavy on your souls!

Hey I'm begging you to listen—look boys, it weren't her that killed them tellers it was me—only me!

Up on the crate, it was that hour before sun, when there was no indication of how close I was to a new morning. I waited for the waiting to break, for the dark of the plain in my face to bring me to dust.

Adela,[1] Primarily Known as The Black Voyage, Later Reprinted as Red Casket of the Heart

by Anon.
1829

We did not understand how she came to be alone. We wished to know more, the more that she alone could tell us. It was well understood in our village that Adela was a beauty, albeit a beauty past her day. But this was of little consequence to us, no?[2]

We came not to spy and discover if indeed her bloom had faded; we came because Mother did not nod to Adela in the street when so rarely she passed, under a parasol despite there being no sun; we came because we knew that on occasion Ad-

---

1 Appears in the French translation as "Alela."

2 The earliest edition attests to a far more implicit positivism, arguably a glass half-full tone, emphasized in the substitution of "yes?" for "no?"

ela had a guest of queer character who alighted in her courtyard well past the witching hour; we came because Father
fumbled to attention when we dared mention our neighbor
"Adela" at supper, piping her syllables into the linen of our
diminutive napkins; and finally, we came because Adela alone
welcomed us: we, the unconsidered, the uninvited, the under
five feet high.

Uncountable afternoons that year, after we had gotten our
gruel[3] —some of us trammeled up with the governess, others,
the tutor—we raced en bloc to the back of beyond, letting ourselves into the bedimmed foyer of Adela's ivy-shrouded, crum-
bling house. She who was alone could not wish to be, yet she
alone had made it so, and we altogether wished to know why.
Fittingly, we slid in our tender, immature fingers to try and pry
Adela open. Perchance she felt this to be a merciless naïveté; as
if we, Edenic formlings, did not yet have the knowledge of our
collective strength.

What is it, the youngest of us ventured to ask, That has
caused you to cloister yourself all through your youth? A
thwarted wish to be a nun or a monk?

It was easy for us to envision Adela pacing down a win-
dowless hall, needlework dragging over stone, her nun's habit
askew.

Her stockinged toes working their way into the topmost
corner of the divan, Adela fluttered in her crinoline. She pressed
the back of her hand to a crimson'd cheek, laughing, Oh dearest children, why it has been years since I have blushed! I sup-

---

3 Here, punishment. There is yet another edition, likely from the turn of
   the century and, as such, establishes that upon meeting the children, Adela
   applies a poultice to their wounds, thereby tinging her kindness with prac-
   tices of the occult.

pose I must confess that it was as lamentable a story as any of you could wish . . .

One with pirates, we asked, One of dead Love and dashed Hope? Then we all at once paused, for her eyes summoned a darkling look as if she had drifted somewhere parlous, somewhere damned.

Pirates? Adela? Pirates?

No, she cried with a toss of her head. The lamp dimmed and the window rattled, lashed by a burst of sudden rain.

Adela, we did chorus, Adela?

Her silhouette bolted upright, Children? The lamplight returned restoring Adela's dusky radiance. You curious cherubs, why it's a foolish tale of romantic woe. I was in love and my love turned out to be quite mad, and well we know, no candle can compare to fire. And so I have chosen to remain alone.

But for us the mystery had only begun. Who was this Unnamed Love? Was he of our acquaintance? Had he wed another? Was his corpse buried in the village graveyard? Was he locked in a madhouse wherein he paced the floors, dribbling "Adela" into the folds of his bloodstained cravat? We wished to know and demanded that she tell us.

Oh, he is quite alive, murmured Adela languidly, pouring herself a glass of Madeira, *meio doce*, to the brim, stirring, spilling it with her little finger, passing the glass around when we begged for a driblet.

Is he married? we asked, our lips stained with wine.

He is not. Though I have heard it said that he is betrothed . . . to a lovely heiress of a small but respectable estate in North Carolina.

We choked on our commutual sip, Won't you stop him if indeed you love him? You will, won't you? Tell us you will, Adela, do!

No indeed. I wish them happy, she said with a deep violet tongue.

We did not think she could mean what she did say. We pressed her as we refilled her glass, Do you love him still? Was it not a lasting attachment?

Oh yes. I'll love him forever. But what of it? she asked.

How was it possible, we mulled aloud, That Love did not rescue the day? Was this not what she had read to us from these very volumes by which we were surrounded? What of *The Mysteries of Udolpho*? Lord Byron's *Beppo*?

Adela nodded in affirmation yet was quick to forewarn, Do not forget the lessons of *Glenarvon!*[4]

But should not Love and Truth strive against aught else, ergo it is better to Perish Alone in Exile? Adela, you must be mistaken, we assured her, the oldest patting the top of her be-jeweled hand, For if your Love knew you loved him in perpetuum, he would return and return in a pig's whisper!

That would be ill-judged, nor would I permit such a thing, she snapped. As I said, he is quite mad and impossible to abide. Please, let us not speak of it, it was all too too long ago.

Adela, we wheedled, Won't you at least tell us the name of your lost love? Don't you trust us, Adela? Why there is nothing you do not know of us! Nothing we have not gotten down on our knees to confess! You know that we borrowed Father's gun

---

4 A Gothic novel by Byron's jilted lover Lady Caroline Lamb, that Byron himself reviled as a "Fuck and Publish" in which the innocent, Calantha (the avatar for Lamb), is seduced by the evil antihero, Glenarvon (a thinly veiled portrayal of Byron). Both Calantha and Lamb were subsequently ruined.

and we shot it; that we broke Mother's vase and we buried it; that we contemplated our governess and tutor in the long grass giving off strange grunts and divers groans till their caterwauling ceased in a cascade of competing whimpers.

Now hush! Didn't I tell you not to speak of that? Very well. His name is Percival Rutherford, she yawned, entreating us to close the blinds.

><

It was a bad plan. A wicked plan. We did not know if it came from us or the Devil so full was it of deceit. At home, milling in the library, in perusal of our aim, we selected a volume of Shakespeare's Comedies, since they all ended in marriage and marriage was by and large our end. The Bard, we suspected, had a number of strategies upon the matter.

We set about with quill and ink and put our nib to paper. Sitting cross-legged on the dais of a desk whilst we huddled below in consternation, the oldest clapped us to attention to declaim, feather aloft:

• Dressing as boys or the boys of us dressing as girls!

We were uncertain as to what this would achieve and thus struck it off.

• Dressing Adela in disguise so that she can visit Percival and get high-bellied!

We were equally uncertain as to whether Adela was past the fecundating age.

• Have Adela rescue her love from a lioness thereby making him everlastingly indebted to her!

While there was no doubt in our collective hearts that Adela could, if put to the test, best a lion—was she not the owner of a mighty sword that hung on her wall belonging to her long-deceased father?—we did doubt we could procure a lioness in this part of the country. The second oldest elbowed their way up to the desk, chastising the oldest for bothering to scribble down a strategy that was so abominably foolhardy. The oldest sneered back that the second was the one with no veritable sense of Byronic ideals. To which the second scoffed, Airmonger! But the oldest merely chose to employ a snub and concluded:

• Fake Adela's death and give Percival report of it? Or! Send a false missive to each, swearing that one loves the other!

Enough, barked the second oldest, crossly claiming that no remedy to our ails could be hit upon in the Comedies. Thus, we began undividedly to search elsewhere in the Canon and quickly fell upon our consensual favorite, *Othello*.[5] We conferred, then confirmed by a show of hands: we must find Adela a beau to make her lost love jealous; Percival, in turn, would wrestle with the arrogance of his tortured soul until goaded into a violent show of love, which would cure him of his madness, whereupon they would be wed, us serving as the bridal party.

---

5   See Mamney, "In works such as Shakespeare's *Othello*, the female character is a canvas onto which the male character ejaculates his fears of emasculation and desire for dominance."

Our unanimous impetus was thus: one day, someday, one by one, we would leave this village and behind us, Adela: a tawny, companionless outcast. This we found insupportable.

>‹

It had come to our attention that the ladies of the village were increasingly fond of the new architect, Mr. Quilby, who had taken a lodging above the apothecary. Our aunts were made prostrate admiring his finely wrought neckties and excellent leg. He is not quite Brummell,[6] the second oldest of us had quipped, not thoroughly convinced of Quilby's suitability let alone his foil status. However, the oldest had been quick to counter that Adela was a spinster by most everyone's calculations—though no lamb dressed in ewe's clothes, with a countenance that was beyond pleasing to the eye—still most of the unattached gentlemen would think her a Tabby. However, Mr. Quilby, the oldest had gone on to expostulate, Has streaks of silver in his sideburns plainly visible. A man of his years will be less concerned by Adela's being a Thornback.[7]

>‹

The following afternoon we tromped through the fields and into the village square, where we found Mr. Quilby at his

6 The reference to Beau Brummell (1778–1840), the innovator of the modern man's suit and inspiration of the Dandy movement, many scholars believe, infers that Quilby will not suffer Brummell's profligate fate of dying penniless and mad.

7 Nineteenth-century audiences suspected that Adela suffered from syphilis. This disease was thought to result in hardened lesions on the trunk, which serves to give a double resonance to "thornback."

drafting table, his sleeves rolled high. Under our arms we had baskets of fresh-baked bread and preserves, for we knew how to be satisfactorily winning children, to lisp and wreathe smiles when such a display was demanded.

Mr. Quilby was intrigued by our description of the enchanting recluse with whom all men dangled and yet no man had ever snared. He quizzed us as to why we thought him the one to win such an elusive prize? Though Quilby admitted he well understood that as the village's newest bachelor, matchmaking mamas would be upon him, he owned he was surprised to find that they would recruit their children to employ such endeavors.

We said in one breath that we believed Adela to be lonely and thought perhaps it would cheer her to have a worthy friend near to her in age in whom she could confide. Quilby, breaking off a chunk of bread said, betwixt his chews, that he was not adverse to such a meeting. The second oldest of us deplored the profusion of Quilby's crumbs, hissing that Quilby was not capable of being the understudy's understudy let alone the rival. But Quilby, unmindful of this sally, inquired, How do you think you could lure such a confirmed hermit?

But we were there well before him. The next evening, the youngest of us was meant to take part in a glee at the chapel, a recital to which Adela had long been promised to attend. In this fashion, was Quilby gulled and the first act of our accursed cabal complete.

➤◄

On the day in question, we were trembling in our boots and slippers, shaking in our corsets and caps, when at long last Adela slipped in at the back of the church. She was a trifle haggard, but we conjectured that if our Star was noticeably dimmed, Quilby would only be made less shy on his approach. In the final applause, the oldest of us mimed to Quilby that he should come make her acquaintance, which Quilby did with a genteel air, bowing and being so courtly as to bestow a light kiss atop Adela's hand. The second of us was obliged to yield an approving nod. That blush which we ourselves had beheld only the other day returned and we pursued it down Adela's throat and across her breasts. Bobbing a sketch of a curtsey, Adela made to turn, fretful for her carriage, but Quilby was quick to inquire, M'am, is it you that lives in the old Nelson place?

Why yes, sir, I am a Nelson. My father passed it on to me when he died.

You see, I am an architect and I thought it quite a rare specimen of local architecture.

Very likely, sir, she mumbled.

M'am, I do wonder if I might take it upon myself to intrude upon you, and pay a visit to view the interior?

Feeling the weight of the eyes of the village bearing down upon her, Adela flung out her consent and fled.

Mother appeared at our sides, peeved we'd been seen speaking to Adela, though she would not shew her displeasure before Mr. Quilby with whom she became something of a coquette.[8]

But we, with the newly acquired address of Percival Rutherford in our combined grasp, sent our hero an invitation for Adela's forthcoming, fictive nuptials to Quilby, thus setting the stage for a disastrous second act.

---

8 This negation of their mother's sexuality is an example of the *male policing* the children engage in to mediate any potentially disruptive female power.

⤜⤛

He was not what we expected. No, he, who burst into Adela's parlor inarticulate and unannounced, in a mode of dress which was slightly outmoded. He, who had not even donned a white, frilled poet's shirt to our thronged disappointment. On first perusal, his chin flapped, his considerable belly paunched and his forehead accordioned. It was a rum go,[9] his hasty shuffling to the pianoforte, where moments before we had been in concert, ranging from soprano to falsetto, the boys of us having dropped neither balls nor voices, while Adela played and Quilby turned pages with gusto.

Adela got to her feet, crying out in wonderment, Percy? But this, too, was a disappointment: an unsatisfactory sobriquet. It would have been better had he been named Orlando or Ferdinand or Rhett, even calling him Rutherford we thought would have more than sufficed.

I apologize for coming without so much as sending my card, but I find I must speak with you, his breaking voice inviting despite the want of delicacy in his manner.

Adela flushed, confirming that we had made no synchronized misstep. Pray Percy, this is—you sir, are unexpected. I have guests.

We sensed it was not us to whom she was referring and used this vexed pause to reexamine our attempt at a retrieved Gallant. Percy did have a thin black mustache of which the second oldest was mightily pleased, and waves of disheveled black hair of which the oldest suspected the application of curl papers, but

---

9   An oblique reference to Percy as a dissolute alcoholic.

we contemporaneously disregarded this, for Percy displayed the requisite lock-clutching. His skin was appropriately pale, a near silky iridescence and we could forgo, on this occasion, to note the plump shadows beneath both his eyes. Lips ruby, chin cleft, sadly brown not blue eyes—yet he was the owner of a fine aquiline nose that any Antony[10] might have had. We would have continued to be encouraged by our mustered précis as we concomitantly plumbed our imaginations in order to restore the bloom of his cankered youth, had not Percy abruptly swooned, causing Adela to bid us: Fetch me the smelling salts!

To this very day, we are haunted by the image of Percy splayed unceremoniously across the divan, his black curls crushed in Adela's lap whilst she wafted him awake. Mr. Quilby, mumpish, hovered, desperate to comment on the impropriety of Percy's head resting so near Adela's nether region. But Quilby bit back his tongue, bided his time and played his part, inquiring, Should a doctor be fetched?

Adela brushed back Percy's hair as he blinked awake and struggled to sit. I do apologize, Percy blenched. I am not altogether well.

Ashley Quilby, declared Quilby coming forth to shake hands, How do you do?

This is Percy Rutherford, said Adela, then looking down meaningfully, Percy, no doubt you are fatigued. Why don't you retire to the guest bedroom while you are thus indisposed?

Percy staggered up, nodding vaguely, his greatcoat slipping to the carpet, his stare fixed but not seeing, a rolling intensity in that mad, reckless eye.

---

10 Yet another veiled barb as to Adela's sexual depravity, for since the success of Emperor Augustus's propaganda machine, Cleopatra has long been portrayed as oversexed.

Percy having taken his leave, Quilby signaled to us. We affected to be admiring the parlor's wood paneling. He then asked Adela with the utmost civility, I take it that he is known to you? Does this gentleman come unannounced often?

Percy is—we were, you see, childhood friends, wavered Adela.

Friends, repeated Quilby.

Well to own the truth, when I was very young and very silly, we almost eloped.

Good God, ejaculated Quilby, laughing.

Adela's smile did not reach her eyes. Yes, well never fear, we were caught by Percy's mother, and we outgrew such . . . pranks.

Quilby asked Adela to take a turn in the garden. She put out her hand, That does sounds agreeable. Will you excuse us, my angels?

Of course, we curtsied and bowed. But as the joint bene-factors of her fortune, we naturally followed, concealing our youthful limbs in the bramble.

Once in the garden, Mr. Quilby pumped her palm, saying, Adela, my darling girl—I mean to say, dear madam—I am com-pelled to confess that since making your acquaintance, I have felt myself enraptured in your presence. This has not happened, nor did I imagine it ever would, since a mild case of calf-love in Virginia almost thirty years ago!

Adela looked pained but primly amused. I thank you. I ex-pect at our age it does seem that it is past all hope.

I suppose it is all too soon but I feel the expediency of—Mr. Quilby dropped to one knee crushing the toes of her slipper and she yelped. Oh sweet heart, forgive me! I am all nerves. Ahem, Quilby cleared his throat, Adela, my pet, I would like permission to pay my addresses to you.

We shuddered in the shrubbery. We had not expected this hasty realization of our fiction. Adela's expression remained bland, as if Quilby had merely inquired about the weather. Eventually, she made a movement, lifting her chin, looking up at what seemed to be the heavens, but we side by side saw to be the guest bedroom window, and with a gleam in her eye, she said: Why, yes.

➤◄

After Mr. Quilby had departed, we stationed ourselves at the parlor windows, which looked out onto the garden. Ensemble'd, we watched Adela while she read, or rather tried in vain to read, flinging down novel after novel. Hearing a heavy tread on the stairs, she paused and we shrank to the sill, pushing the windows open an inch. Percy came striding through the parlor doors, promptly accosting her, So he's the man you are going to marry? Foisting himself upon her where she lay curled on the divan, he lifted up her skirts to administer some tutor-like touching, from which Adela, no governess, tore away.

You're being a dead bore, she cuffed him.

I find myself unable to resist, came his protest.

You hypocrite, Adela said. What would your betrothed have to say to this vulgarity?

Percy began to turn wildly about the parlor. I don't care! I got the invitation!

Adela watched him from beneath heavy lids. What invitation? You haven't changed. Do I not have a right to happiness after all this time? I'm not a girl in the first blush of youth.

But I am meant to be the one, Percy sobbed, tearing at his corkscrews.

We, Adela included, were similarly disconcerted; we did not expect that our Gallant should blub.

Pray Percy, don't be vexed. How did you get here? she asked, leading that sad romp[11] back to the divan.

Putting his head on her shoulder, the ramshackle Percy wiped his nose against her sleeve. I suppose you'll think it ill-judged of me, but I borrowed my mother's carriage, he said.

Your dibs out of tune[12] again? she asked.

Percy shrugged, tracing the plunging neckline of Adela's gown. I'm at a stand save for Mother's coin. She leaned back languidly, watching the movement of his fingers. Percy slipped a hand between cloth and flesh. Is that it, Adela, he groped, pinching, You're marrying that man for his money?

Adela was rueful with an air of recklessness we had never witnessed. Pooh, I'm not going to keep correcting you. Though Quilby is a kind, most obliging man. One could not wish for more. In a husband.

Percy kissed down the side of her neck. I may not have Quilby's fortune, Adela, but you shall always be She and I am He.

Adela seemed to collect herself and fobbed him off. Oh, fetch me a drink.

He spied the Madeira, Your father's brand? You think me

---

11 This trope was frequently used to denote a "wild child," however in the context of the Byronic hero discourse, the children are referring to the acute chronic melancholy of Percy's ruttish dissipation.

12 Adela is revealing that, by bringing his agenda of disharmony upon her, Percy is threatening to dismantle her authenticity with his financial cacophony.

a fool but I will not let you get away with this, he growled, pouring.

Behind the window, our mouths were watering.

Whatever do you mean? she stood and we ducked.

I won't, he said and polished off the Madeira, holding out an emptied glass. If your precious Quilby knew what you really are, do you think he would still countenance the nuptial?

Nuptial? Stop it. You wouldn't. Adela filled his glass and handed it to him but not before dipping in her little finger.

But I would, he countered. Depend upon it. Percy took that finger in his mouth and suckled. Adela tried to pull away.

She frowned. Your mother would not permit us to be together now as she did not permit it then.

Percy threw her hand from him: O blast your secret! tossing his glass in the fire, almost rousing us to burst into applause. He shall not have you! our summoned Gallant roared and flew up the stairs, leaving Adela with the arduous task of picking up hundreds of shards of glass.

This too was not what we had expected. Adela had a secret. And this secret was spoiling our plot. We bunched under a marble cherub to consider a concurrent abandoning of ship. But the second oldest leapt up on the angel's knee, a hand round its marble neck and holding a penknife high, condemned us roundly as traitors to the cause, rasping, We must needs rally! Each of us must take a blood vow to help Adela no matter what the twist!

Hand in hand, we solemnly rose to the penknife and were poked, suckling our little fingers as hard as any Percy. In line unbroken, we marched and orbited Adela who was still kneeling in the shards.

Weep no more, we have come! But before we tell you the

wrongs we wish to undo, you must tell us, Adela, what is your secret? What are you?

Adela brushed her mussed dress with shaky fingers. Oh no. Oh my dears . . . You see, my father, was not a gentleman but a pirate, and he saved Percy's father's life. His sole request was that Percy's father keep watch over me, his motherless daughter born on the wrong side of the blanket. Yes. That Merry-begot[13] was myself.

Till then we had never met a Two-legged Tympany![14] We inspected her anew for signs. Why did your father jilt your mother? Was it at the altar, we asked, our eyes filling with the image.

Adela turned to gaze into the fire, muttering, It is abominable that this should happen now. I thought I should be safe! Oh but why did I ever hope to escape?

Will you toss Quilby aside, Adela? we asked rubbing our hands together. You must! The second oldest averred, Quilby will certain not want you, Adela, if you are a base-born.

But Mr. Quilby has been all tenderness. Dear children, please be kind, please endeavor to understand what you cannot possibly . . .

We moved as one to tug her skirts but exchanged this tactic for a rough shake. Percy knows your secret and still loves you, Adela! We will go and fetch him and he will whisk you away!

No, she cried, You will not! I will not!

Is there something more that you are not telling us? we inquired.

---

13 Such vernacular as "merry"-ness suggests that Adela's "merry" sexual misconduct has been enjoyed since birth.

14 Note the children's conception of Adela's bastardy approaches deformity.

No, don't be silly, little ones, she said.

You would unburden all to us, wouldn't you? You wouldn't want to wound us by keeping more secrets. Mother might ask what we've been up to all day and why we look so blue-deviled. It makes us ever so sad that you do not trust us as we thought. Why, we are positively sick! we choked. We're about to have spasms! On cue, the youngest of us started sobbing. Oh won't Mother wonder why all our eyes are so red, why our complexion is so wan? Shall we unburden ourselves to her, Adela, shall we?

Adela stared at us as if we she hardly knew. I am so tired, she said in a strangled voice not quite her own. No. Don't, please. I will tell you. I will have done.

We laid on our fronts, our chins on our fists, rapt to receive!

My father was a tawny-moor[15] of the West Indies and because of it, Percy's mother would not allow us to be married. He is badly dipped and lives practically on her purse-strings.

We will here divulge that we were jointly taken aback. We had never seen the daughter of a tawny-moor before, let alone stood in the daughter of a tawny-moor's library. We did not desire to think of Adela differently, but we could not deny that she had become someone quite Other.

You have been unfaithful to us, Adela, we quavered and asked if we could touch the hair of a black base-born.

She lowered her head, saying, But you must believe that I had no intention of breaking your trust.

---

15 *Adela*, lighting the way for *Wuthering Heights*, is known to have thoroughly inspired Charlotte Brontë to pay homage in the creation of Heathcliff, the construction of Moor as man, allowing Brontë to position the subaltern as the vessel of violent agency.

The oldest of us traced her cheek as if a slight swarth should rub off.[16] Our fingers fingering her, the second oldest speculated, Her moorness merely lends her character—the secret was only an error in judgment. And she does not look yellow-pined, the oldest approvingly replied. No indeed, she is perfectly fair, the second urged and concluded, Why the curtain is not down, but we are in another tale entirely!

All the while Adela stood, unmoving, watching us from far back in her eyes.

However, we all must agree she is metamorphose'd[17] and that for this she must suffer, the oldest said feverishly kissing her hand in the manner of a Percy.

Adela flushed, snatching it away rigidly, How dare you! Do not touch me! You are but still in the Nursery!

The oldest climbed on Adela's desk, clapping us to attention, declaiming, quill aloft:

• Suiciding by poison or suiciding by knife!

We were dubious as to what this would achieve and thus we struck it off.

• Bake her children in a pie, then invite her to the feast!

---

16 This fluidity in their conception of race typically predates the nineteenth century and is most often found in the eighteenth century, when skin color was a less fixed secondary identity marker. For a charming and oft incisive exploration of this, see Roxann Wheeler's *The Complexion of Race: Categories of Difference in Eighteenth-Century British Culture.*

17 A Creole female, which Adela has now claimed as her identity, was commonly depicted in the discourse of white colonial domination as lascivious and unstable due to the West Indian heat.

Not only did Adela not have children, but we were uncertain as to whether we wanted to be in a Revenge Tragedy.

• Be strangled, be drowned, have her eyes gouged out?

While there was no doubt in our collective minds that Adela could, if put to the test, achieve a nobly gory end, we did not know how to go about it.

The youngest of us tripped forward, opening *Troilus and Cressida*. Zounds! cried the oldest, Adela'd make a beautiful prisoner of war. We can sell her and our early idyllic notion of the ownership of love will remain ours evermore. False as Cressid, concurred the second.

Just then Percy, the Percy whom we ourselves had procured, whom we had selected as the hero of our hobbyhorse,[18] leaned in the door with a pistol cocked. You naughty children, he smiled yet snarled. Now since you are so anxious to be a part of Adela's fate, I will prevail upon you all to tie up my darling girl with the curtain cord.

We shall not, we sputtered. We haven't sold the Negress so she is not yours!

The Devil she isn't! He shrieked, lifting the pistol.

Percy, you fool, they are but children! Adela exclaimed.

Percy pointed his gun at us. I suspect it is these brats who have entrapped you. I wouldn't have taken you for such a milksop, Adela. O my sweet martyr, Percy cackled. My little devils, shall you help your bit of ebony to her cross?

---

18 This carries the connotation of Percy's animalistic virility astride Adela's noble savagery. See Dowd, whose *Barbarous Beasts, White Toys, and Hybrid Paternities: Considerations on Race and Sexuality in the Caribbean* examines these tensions.

We did not want to do it but we altogether did; the sum of us helped the villain. Adela offered us no violence, not even when some of us, being fascinated by her whimper, tightened the cord so that it bit into her breast.

So my underlings, how would you choose this story to end? Love or Death? Percy pointed the barrel at the oldest: You, choose.

The oldest of us looked to the rest of us, but we shook our heads, having come to no unanimous answer. We had not had the time to parley.

Come child, let me see how well Adela has magicked[19] you, he said.

L-l-love? stuttered our oldest and the rest of us, knowing it necessary, absolutely necessary, to preserve an absolutely unified front, followed suit: Love! Love! Love!

Percy crowed. Well I do believe Love has conquered all. Adela, my sweet, Percy congratulated her wryly, You have taught them so well.

Not I, replied Adela. For I would have chosen Death.

Don't be such a ninnyhammer, spat Percy, shaken.

No, she corrected, You cannot think me so chicken-hearted. All these years I have done without you, what makes you suppose I should want your uneven tyranny now?

All were silent. Then Percy drawled: It would be best to gag her mouth, she's ruining my arc. We, wrenching down more curtain rope, pushed it into the wetness of her mouth.

However, Quilby, unheralded, unexpected, taking us by unawares, burst into the parlor, bellowing in horrified ac-

---

19 This accusation hearkens to the seemingly fixed, misogynist association between West Indian women and black magic which was stereotypical during the period in which "Adela" was composed.

cents, Adela, my poor girl! Damme, what has this blackguard
done?

She's a black base-born and she wants Death! we shouted.

Quilby's eyes fairly started out of his head. She is God's
creature, he said, throwing off his coat then loosening his cravat. And you shall not harm her.

The two men, prodigiously embroiled in fisticuffs, grappled
at each other, vying for the pistol. Adela worked furiously to
extricate her wrists and, once free, pulled down her gag, crying,
No you shall not! rushing toward Percy. And we, en masse, ran
as one toward Death, wedding our wee bodies with hers, until
her, our, their fingers wrapped about the pistol.

O Adela, though we now know the Why, that How is
known solely by those individual fingers which pulled the lone
trigger. We only know presently, and indeed knew then, that
he[20] looked more elegant in death than we ever knew him to
be in life, or even when we first had collaboratively imagined
entangling him.

We, no longer the children we have been, have never forgotten that, no matter what shade the skin, the blood is always red.
And for this denouement, we beg you, Adela, to forgive.

Finis.

---

20 In the first German translations, it is curious to note that "she" rather than
"he" dies.

Accidental

At Black Creek, the water is the color of tea, mosquitoes bite and sand soaks through our motel towels. I look for snakes—water moccasins—the man I met at the Super 8 in Picayune says you can smell them coming. I don't smell anything but my mother's Oil of Olay on my face. In the water, just like on her skin, it smells of sweet almonds. Though my legs are already lesioned with bites, I swim to where it's deepest, where the branches of broken trees swirl. Afternoons like these, I wish I lived in the time of Mark Twain, floating down the river in a canoe, reckless about insects and reptiles, armed with a shotgun and a short life expectancy.

After our swim, he drives me to the Flea, empty except for us and the two hags that run it. I'm not saying I'm better than them, but I do have all my teeth. I slip between the racks of forsaken clothes—shrunk, stained, pilled—and use a bent comb on my wet hair in a warped mirror at the back.

Out front, he asks me where I want to go next. He has dull

teeth beginning to brown, and though he isn't bad-looking and offers to buy me lunch, it'll be best if he doesn't know where I'll be staying while I'm in Hattiesburg, so I ask for a ride to the graveyard rather than a local motel.

He looks at me sideways because no one new has been buried there since 1926, but even the long dead need a social call, and there was something downright elegant about mourning in the nineteenth century: the baroque epitaphs where death comes in sleep, by icicle, through a glorious, perilous fall from a swing. On the drive there, he plays the radio too loud, and I'm glad of an excuse not to talk. Coming to Mississippi to track down my father is a gamble, but I am not relying on luck.

As soon as his car pulls up to the graveyard, I shoulder my bag and hop out.

"Hey, if you could— " he strains through the passenger window with a ducked head, cigarette dangling from his lips, a freckled hand leaning on the gearshift.

But I am already standing more than a couple of steps away from the curb on the steaming cemetery grass. "Appreciate you," I nod and walk off. My mother says leaving is my art form, but I think I'm losing my flair.

⌐

The graveyard is hilly and dotted with Confederate flags. Masonic squares and compasses etched every five stones or so. I sit down with a book by an *Esther* and wait for my underwear to dry.

Two hundred years ago, if a family member died, I would have had to prepare their body. The flesh would have literally come into my hands, and I would experience their death with all my senses. I would have to wash and dress them, plug their orifices, prop their mouth shut, rouge their cheeks, and arrange them on a bed as if they were asleep—as if in a few hours they would wake up and ask me something, or ignore me where I was sitting drinking coffee. But after a few hours I would see that their eyelids were unwilling, and would feel the torpidity in their face so that then I could be past avoiding their death and into the full heart of grief.

I myself have only seen one dead body. The woman was my age, my height, my build. Both of us had brown hair, both did a brief stint in real estate, both dropped out of community college. She left school after a year, and I stopped midway. I am an only child, and she was the oldest but an only child for the first nine years. We both loved to swim and each once lived by the water, she in Cape May, me in Pensacola; as kids we took swimming lessons at our community rec centers since neither of our mothers could afford anything private. The year before she was killed, she took surfing lessons in Costa Rica; I took one ten years ago in Galveston with my stepbrother, Hank. In court for vehicular manslaughter, I didn't look as the woman's sister spoke of the family's online memorial page, after prison I watched the page fill and in one photo, I swear we have the same jacket.

Here's where we start to diverge. She was newly divorced and had no children, while I had a baby at fifteen and never married. But when I stood near her still-breathing body, waiting for the ambulance to come, I felt we were interchangeable. It could've been me in her blind spot.

Near evening, I hitch a ride to a motel along the highway. But some people are not as decent as the freckled guy. Some people are encouraged by my size, since as a small woman, even at thirty-seven, from far away I could look like a child. And so some people force you to reveal as you pretend to root in your bag for a tissue with your left hand, the little pistol that you are now holding comfortably in your right. These red-thick ball-cappers need to sense that, as my mother said when she gave me the gun, that you wanna use it, that you've been waiting to use it on any motherfucker dumb enough to be dumb. These people, you see, can only understand humanity at gunpoint. As I walk away from him down the highway, the driver calls me a cuntfaced bitch out his window, detailing my impending bodily harm, but I think he now knows that I too have fears, hopes, dreams.

⌐

I go to see a friend of the family, or it would be more correct to say *a friend of my father's*, and am pleased to discover that Lonnie has a new wife. We sit on his unelevated porch outside Hattiesburg, my hand over my cup to keep out the bugs. It is hard to tell what is hotter, the air or the coffee.

Lonnie's new wife, Carly, is highlighted blond with nails pearled pink: they gleam lilac in the edging sun burning our shins. Though he's old enough to be both of our fathers, she is suspicious, and I'd like to reassure her that I have no designs on Lonnie, who even at the age of sixty-seven likes to go downtown to the old train depot and busk, singing Johnny Cash, Loretta Lynn, some Woody Guthrie. His long hair grows out from the bottom half of his bald head like an evil monk. He's ugly, which is why he always wears aviators. Says it makes the ugly rugged.

He doesn't understand what I am doing here. "This is not your South anymore."

"No, but I have come," I say, "to borrow it again. I'm only living in Virginia at my mom's while she's sick, and once she's doing better who knows where I'll be?"

"How's your boy? How's Levi doing? Is he rising to the occasion?"

I think about my son while I sip my coffee. "He's having a hard time with it, so I can't say he's much help. He doesn't like hospitals."

"How old is he now?"

"He'll be twenty-two in October."

Lonnie grunts. "That's what comes of not having a father figure."

My eyes meet his. "By that you mean Hank?"

"I mean any man."

"Well, I'm okay with hospitals, and I'll be back there soon enough. After I find Dad."

"That's what you come to Hattiesburg to find?"

"That and a land without a mall."

When I was a kid I lived with my father every summer, which I associate with blackened hot dogs, mothers threatening to break their children's legs, rain-sad bean bags in the plastic ruin of back yards, unicorn and Elvis icons on tilted shelves, ghost stories told on rusting merry-go-rounds, sunburnt stallion men named Bubba shoveling potato salad, and peeing in the basement of the Lodge after passing through a gauntlet of suck-cheeked old men in trucker caps. It was a hellish kind of heaven. I wore what I wanted (hot pink, white cotton T-shirts, bikinis); ate what I wanted (cereal, pepperoni pizza, chocolate milk shakes, chicken fingers, ketchup sandwiches); and played all day (spies, kickball, tag) and stayed up till morning reading all night (*Anne of Avonlea, James and the Giant Peach, Island of the Blue Dolphins*).

Lonnie and my father played baseball together at the Lodge. On those weekends, my father and whatever woman was holding court would bring me to the games in the back of their pickup truck beside two coolers of beer and box wine. At night in the parking lot, win or lose, I would lay in the truck bed sucking back sodas and eating candy, watching as the drunks mooned each other until I passed out sugar-drowned under the stars.

My father was a nervy man who leaned more toward a domineering antagonism than violence. Most of the time we got on, as long as I didn't talk too smart. I saved confessionals for my mother. Sometimes in the mornings I would catch him looking at me while I lay in the hammock reading, one dirty foot thrown over doing the rocking, and he'd shake his head as if wondering whose kid I really was. But I had his brown hair and brown eyes and his Sicilian skin that went gold in the sun.

"Do you know where he is?" I ask Lonnie. "His phone's been disconnected."

"Well, he ain't dead . . ." Lonnie waits, "but he might as well be. It's been hard to keep in touch. He missed the wedding, said he'd been in the hospital. Of course that's the drinking. You know how he goes through his phases. A few months back I saw him at the golf course. I'm guessing he still lives off Old Highway 49 with that woman"—he turns to his woman—"what's her name? Kathleen? Darlene?"

"Kim," Carly says, recrossing her legs.

"Yeah, that's the one."

My father has been married three times. To my mother,

then to Hank's mother, and to my mother again. Problem is, he and my mother are still married. I explain to Lonnie that my mother keeps mailing the divorce papers that my father promises to sign but somehow never does. Before she got sick, she hired a process server who had no luck and tried to get a court order to have the notice published in the paper, but the judge denied it, saying she hadn't done enough to find him.

"So now she's sent you," Lonnie says.

"I have a better chance of finding him than anyone else," I say, picking a gnat out of my coffee.

"But what does it matter now?" Lonnie asks.

"Ever since she got sick, it's been bothering her, keeps her up some nights. I think she just wants to be done with him. She says it would give her relief."

"I can understand that." Carly nods.

Lonnie shrugs. "Maybe he'll want to marry that Kim instead."

Kim is a frosted, compulsive tanner who's about sixty. She and my father stay in whatever town until the last casino kicks them out, and then they pack up their camper, and it's on to the next. For eleven years, he's been dragging around this toxic woman who breaks up his every relationship except with their two dogs.

At first, I tried to befriend Kim. When she sent me a silver bracelet for my birthday, I called to thank her, and she told me that my father had begun drinking again. I sighed and said: "I am gonna kill that man." When she got off the phone she started bawling, telling my father I said I wished he were dead. Ten minutes later, he called me up yelling. How easily he believed it.

We turn to look at the wind chimes on Lonnie's porch floating out a stain-glassed tune.

"You wanna stay here while I drive Carly up to Memphis to visit her kids?" he asks.

"I'm all right." I put my emptied cup down. "I was thinking I might stay near Hank."

"That boy's the last thing you need."

"That boy is forty. And Dad . . . Dad must be seventy now. This could be the last time I see him."

"Might could be," Lonnie says, his eyes trying to tell me something I cannot know yet.

But he needn't worry. When I go looking for Dad, I don't go expecting to find a father. We have no relationship, only a joint claim on a past.

⌐

We are the children of the white sands, though we are no longer children and seem to know less. On the walk from my motel room to Hank's truck, his eyes light up like I'm something to see and I'm fifteen again, unfilled in all the right places.

Hank's on a buttload of painkillers and a new antianxiety. He complains his shoulder's acting up, so he drives with one arm; the wind thinning what's left of his auburn hair. He doesn't know where to put me because he's back with his girlfriend, so he's driving me to a motel near him in Slidell.

Says he's gotten fat and likes it. Says when you're fat, food tastes better. I listen to him explain that he still cheats on his girlfriend. Even though now he makes a concerted effort not to. Of course, Hank would never use the word *cheat*.

"I've never called her my girlfriend," he says in the truck outside the motel whose broken sign holds a piece of notebook paper saying $29.99 A Night.

"I'm sure that's how she knows she's not," I say.

"We've had lots of talks about my issues," he says. "It's not something I keep secret."

I tie my hair back. "Good for you. Lemme have a few of those painkillers before I go."

"For what? I know it sounds crazy, darlin, but I'm not as bad as I used to be."

I shrug. "I have sore armpits. Maybe it's arthritis or breast cancer."

"Baby, that's anxiety. I'll give you one of these other things." He opens the faded gym bag that sits between us.

I swallow one dry then open the passenger door. "Do you think, if things had gone differently, we could've been happy together?"

His eyes down, he shakes three pills from a plastic sandwich bag. "Wouldn't have been the worst thing in the world. What're you doing tomorrow?"

"Going out to that trailer park in Gautier Lonnie told me about and see if Dad's there."

"Why didn't you rent a car at the airport? You short on money?"

"Why, you got some to lend me?" I climb out of the truck.

When I look back, he's staring at me. "Don't tell me you're hitching. From Virginia? Lucinda, that's not okay."

I smile at my name. He's the only one who doesn't call me Lucy. "I flew into New Orleans then got some rides the rest of the way." I shut the door and walk up the motel's concrete steps. But on the balcony, I stop and dangle over. "Hey."

He puts down the window. His green eyes are dreaming. "Hey."

Inside his face is the face I knew. "Come up here."

"I don't think that's a good idea," he says.

"You have to," I say.

⌐

Morning. Unquiet at the motel. My brain vigilant and my body consumptive. It does not help that I wake with the train. Between four and five A.M., the locomotive's blare casts a pall over any optimism I might have been storing up for the coming day. Lying next to Hank in the dark morning of the night, I imagine all the ways my life could've gone, which turns into thinking about the best way to shut off my brain. But I would never do that to my son.

I get up and look at the pictures in my wallet. The first is of Levi. He's little here. Maybe six or seven. The picture has a white border and is sunlight saturated. He's wearing a red life jacket and behind him is a gold radiance of lake. The edges are curling, one corner bent having spent 730 days under my pillow.

Levi might have green eyes like Hank, but he has his own face. Though he's about to be twenty-two, long and lean, a hood always over his head, he still has the penitent soft regard he had when he was eight. At that age he was a boy who couldn't fall asleep until the grown-ups did, who tried to stay awake because he was afraid of the moon.

We're not close. At this hour I can admit that. I'm barely his mother in more than name. I know he's a good kid even if he gets high listening to reggae, believes in government conspiracies, and is considering joining the Marines. Even though he's at that age where the smallness of his compassion pinches.

Hank sleeps like a teenager who's still growing. Around six,

I wake him up so he can get home before his girlfriend leaves for work. He rushes into the bathroom and runs the sink. I hear violent splashing.

After last night's pills, my color feels high and my scalp tight. There is a taste in my mouth I don't like. I want to take a cold shower, change my underwear then pack up before the knock of housekeeping and be on my way to Gautier.

Hank comes out of the bathroom saying he needs to pick up coffee because he and his girlfriend are running low. The motel light does bad things to his hair. I don't say much because I am remembering the rules of the way this goes. He sits, busy packing his gym bag until he gets up to hug. His hug makes me smell of him. He's always worn too much deodorant.

When I go into the fluorescent-lit bathroom he comes to the door but not so I can see him. "Aren't you leaving?" I ask my face under the gray film over the mirror.

"Are you upset?"

"Why would I be?" I look older today.

"I just don't know that I could have ever given you what you want," he says into the door frame.

I tie my hair up for a shower and flip on the overhead fan.

"You need money?" he asks. "I don't like you hitching. I can give you some money for a rental. How's three hundred?"

I almost laugh. "Don't worry about me." I pull a stiff, chlorined towel from the rack and lay it across the top of the toilet.

"You think I should send some to Levi? I'm doing all right now."

"She'll be late for work if you don't hurry."

Even with the shower and fan I can hear the door slam.

When I was fourteen my father married Hank's mother, and moved in with them.

In June, I came for my visit. Hank was the star running back on his high school team. He barely fit through the door but was as yielding as he could be. And he was pretty. No one else would ever say they couldn't stop thinking about me.

In July, we stole his mother's car and ran away. He probably imagined we'd be gone a few days, I thought forever. We lasted a month, running out of money in Florida. That last week we parked out in Destin where we slept in the car and lived on the beach. The bikinis got to Hank. The water got to me. I was sent home to my mother pregnant, and she was irate, even when it turned out that Hank would only be my stepbrother for another few weeks.

I put on the socks I thieved from the Flea and start walking toward the highway. I'm a little worried about money. I'm only spending when I'm on the road. I know that as soon as I'm done here I should go right back to my mother's in Virginia and get a job, but ever since I was in prison, I've tried in vain to make myself do the things that ought to be done. Of course I have held various jobs: convenience store clerk, waitress, organic farmer (well a brief spell in Mexico where I was paid in food and shelter), but it is so hard to live in the place where everyone knows your shame.

I'm close to Highway 59 when Hank's truck pulls up on the side of the road and he heaves himself out, wearing his glasses. "Get in," he says, "I'm taking you to Gautier."

"Your girlfriend's gonna leave your ass for good."

He wipes his wet hair off his forehead. "I don't want you hitching—it ain't the sixties."

"Are you high?" I move my bag, which has begun cutting into my shoulder.

"Not more than usual."

Every few years either Hank or I try to get back together. It never works much past a week's delirious phone calls and a fevered meet up in an overpriced motel. Hank knows me like nobody does, but when we're together everything seems to escalate in a bad way.

I get in the truck and turn to him, his eyes look glazed behind his lenses. "You can't drive," I say, "you're drunker than Cooter Brown."

He waves me off. "I'm fine. Just had some bourbon. Top shelf. I had to get to it before her."

"It's nine-thirty."

"It's been a busy morning." He goes to start the ignition.

I put my hand over his keys. "I'm not riding with you in this condition."

"Goddamn it, Lucinda, don't be so puritanical. Do you want to go to Gautier or not?" He throws up his hands. "You drive then."

I grab my bag from the floorboard. "I'll get myself there. I don't need you to come with me."

He turns in his seat. "You must have your damn license back by now."

I shake my head. "I don't." I hesitate. "I haven't driven since the accident."

He stares at me. "But it's got to have been fifteen years or more . . . How did you meet me last year in Alabama?"

I look at the dust on the toes of my boots. "I took a bus and then I took a cab."

He massages his eyes under his glasses. "Look, it'll be fine, honey. You'll remember. It'll all come back to you."

The night the woman that I killed died was cloudy, rainless, overhead a mystery of sky. It was September and I wanted to be close to my youth and the secret purity of death. I walked my mother's acres spilling my second beer and communing with the trees. When I started my car it was two in the morning. She was leaving a bar at the exact same time. As I drove, the night swelled and pulled black before me. I went too fast because I felt I had to. I broke her chest because I didn't see.

"Lucinda?"

I hug my bag and close my eyes.

"Darlin, I'll be right here if you forget."

I hear Hank get out of the truck and walk around, then open the passenger door. "Scoot over," he says. I don't move. He puts a warm hand on the side of my face and says in my ear: "Do it for your mother."

I take a deep breath, let go of the bag and slide over. I adjust the seat so I'm closer to the wheel. I turn the keys too hard and the engine sounds angry. Then I push my foot down on the brake and my right hand moves us from park. Next is the gas and if my body will obey, we go backward.

⌐

My father's not at the trailer park, but his neighbors remember him. They seem to think he moved to one in Mobile. They said Kim was with him and left behind a birdcage and two plastic flamingoes, which Hank and I decline to retrieve.

By the time we reach the trailer park in Mobile where the land has no trees and everything is blasted desolate by the sun, it's late afternoon. Hank's girlfriend has been calling him, but he hasn't answered. He just looks down at his phone, watching it tremble. I wonder how much longer he'll hold out.

When we pull up, my father is sitting on the crooked porch

steps, hugging his knees to his chest like a boy exhausted from swimming. He's in cutoff jeans, holding a tallboy and when he sees who's in the truck, he comes off the porch to greet us in the gravel drive, his walk an agile stagger. I can tell that he's coming off a bender the way his grainy eyes pucker. Kim stays at the kitchen window making fried chicken, and he doesn't invite us in.

"Hey now." He gives me a rub on the back and shakes Hank's hand. "Didn't expect to see you two. Tweedle Dee"—he taps my head and, eyeing Hank—"Tweedle Dumb."

Hank drags three plastic chairs over the dirt coming up through the grass.

"Y'all staying in Mobile?" My father sits and his cartoon tattoos distend over his belly. Somehow you can see his ribs and the man still has a gut.

"I've come here looking for you, Dad."

He squints at me, annoyed, like I'm yelling. "Well, now you found me." He looks away.

I decide to try for sweetness. "What happened to your phone? You need a bill paid or something?"

"Don't offer him nothing," says Hank.

"Naw, I don't need to be wasting my money. It's Kim that likes gabbing on the phone, not me. Let her waste hers. How long's it been, girl? You look exactly the same. But you, Hank, you put on some weight, boy."

"It's been about three years, Dad," I say.

He looks at me with yellowed brown eyes. "Three years? You must not have seen this, then. We bought this here." He waves proudly behind him at the flimsy butter-green trailer.

"Where'd you get the money for that, Carl?" asks Hank.

"Counting cards at Blackjack."

"But you can't pay for your damn phone bill?"

"Leave it, Hank," I tell him. "I got something important to say to you, Dad."

"Hey he ain't knock you up again, did he?"

Hank is on his feet, his plastic chair toppled over. Behind him is a row of mailboxes with crosses on top.

"Hank," I stand, my arm out, "the man is seventy—he's too old to fight."

Hank glares at him. "He ain't too old to start one."

My father doesn't bother getting up, but all his old effrontery is mottled sublimely in his face. "I'll be in my grave before you get a hit over me." He turns and spits in the dust near my feet. "Girl, you come all the way out here just to tell me some bad damn news? Well go on then. Who'd you kill this time? What-ever it is I ain't paying for it. Even if I had the money, and I don't."

Like a switch has been thrown, my eyes fill.

"I knew it'd be like this," Hank says. "You want me to beat the shit out of him?"

"Dad," I say, my throat tight, "we're going."

"That's y'all's decision." My father crosses his arms over his chest.

Hank steps in front of me, saying under his breath, "What about your momma?"

When my mother told me on the phone that she had stage four cancer, I stubbed out my cigarette in the green curl of my apartment complex's front yard, but smoke continued to rise from the butt like it was rising from the ground. She asked me to come home and take care of her and I wanted to say no. I have barely taken care of anybody, not myself, not even Levi. He was seven when I first left. For the two years I was in, I wouldn't let her bring him to the prison. After I got out, I owed the state, the hospital, and couldn't look at anyone who knew me, and so I left again.

I take the papers out from my bag and hand them to my father. "Mom needs you to sign these."

He looks at them and immediately gets red. "I ain't signing anything."

I open my bag again, taking out the gun. "Then I need you to sign those."

Hank tries to grab my arm, but I step away. "Hank, you can wait in the truck, but I'm not leaving without him signing."

"You better not do anything crazy, you being a felon." My father grins, but his eyes are boiling.

"Hank, give him the pen."

My father glares at the pen in Hank's hand. "You're forcing me illegally? Under duress?"

"That's right, Dad, criminal that I am."

"It's a shame that a child would pull a gun on her own father. I want you to know Kim's in there calling the police."

Hank is looking from me to my father to Kim in the kitchen window. I don't look at the trailer, even the thought of this terrifies me. "I don't care," I say.

"I don't think you have the balls to use it." My father gestures to the little pistol.

I lift it from his chest to his head. "But you wouldn't be the first person I've killed, right?"

"Honey," Hank says, "we can figure out a better way to do this."

"If I did sign," says my father, "and I'm not saying I will, I want the two of you to never come round here again."

"Carl, why would we want to, with you always poking old wounds?" says Hank, disgusted.

My father looks at me, hands on his hips. "Why does she want me to sign it now?"

"Because she's sick. Because she's dying and she doesn't want to die as your wife. She might live another year, but then she's gone." The tears come now, fat and terrible. "And we'll never see her again. There won't be an again. So we have to say yes to whatever she wants, to whatever she asks me and you."

"Of what?" My father demands, running a hand through his gray hair. "She's dying of what?"

I gesture at Hank and wipe my face with my shirt. "Cancer," Hank says.

"So please sign it," I say. "Please. It's what she wants."

My father takes the pen and leaning on Hank's back, signs the papers in his uneven scrawl. Hank takes them and looks them over. I let the gun drop, but can't bring myself to put it back in my purse. As I walk to the truck, my legs jelly, desperate to sit and hide in that hot metal space away from the light, Kim comes out onto the porch and in the snap of the screen I hear my father say, "You think you'd feel these things." Said to himself as if he were an actor who finally finds he is alone onstage.

⌐

Hank drives us to Panama City and parks in front of the beach. He buys a bottle of Canadian whiskey and we lie out in the truck bed. I take off my boots and he rubs my feet. It's warm but there's a merciful thick breeze.

"Can I ask you something?" Hank props himself up on an elbow.

"Why not?" I take a drink from the bottle and curl my back on his chest.

"Why'd you wait so long to tell Levi I was his father?"

"I don't know." I shrug deeper into his body. "Mom always said it was better that way. She thought it would be confusing for him since you were my stepbrother."

He sits up. "That again? It wasn't even for a year."

"But still." Above, the stars are too many to count.

"If he'd known I could've done more." Hank lifts the bottle from me. "You think I should've done more?"

"I don't know," I say, but I do know.

He takes a long drink. "It's not looking like I'm gonna have me any other kids, which means Levi's my only son and what have I done for him?"

I take back the bottle, tracing its mouth with my finger, round and round. "When I was a little girl, sometimes at church they'd skip the service and stage Judgment. You never knew whether Mrs. Monroe in the starring role of Jane, or Mr. Daniels playing Lance were gonna be damned or resurrected based on the measure of their various sins until the angels or devils came to take them. But who took them was never the worst part, it was the waiting."

He leans forward, looking down at me. "You saying it's too late?"

I sit up and try to find where the night meets the water. "The truth is my mom does everything—did everything for him anyway."

"But I feel bad, Lucinda," Hank says. "Could you maybe tell her that? I want her to know, I really do, that I feel so bad." He sinks back until he's lying flat.

When Levi was born, I didn't want to be a mother. I thought I would, or hoped I would later. I don't wish that it didn't happen, I only wish it had happened differently.

In the morning, the beach is empty except for a couple of joggers. Hank and I strip naked and race each other down the hot white sand to the breaking waves. We are happy, we are frightened, and we are not saved.

The Diplomat's Daughter

Natalia used to be a wife. His name was Erik. His name was Viggo. His name was Christien. His name was Lucas. His name was Nils.

He hit her. They had no children. He drove a motorcycle. Ran a company. Was a pastor, a surfer, an accountant. He taught her how to shoot, to drink, to bleed. Her husband. Her boss. Her man. See her as student, as interpreter, as waitress. See her learning how to skin: you start at the neck, then you dig into the hide, into the cooling fat, and pull away from what lived.

She had a missionary zeal he did not give her. It was a fatalistic streak he admitted from the start was hers. He was, you see, a Calvinist at heart.

"Erik," she asked, "am I ready?"

"No," he joked, scratching his beard. "It's Christien."

Christien.

When she spoke that name always her voice hid behind her.

What he did to her was done to them all. There was an essential equality in their small company. But she could admit she was the favorite. Though attention is not always a benefit. In some cases, it merely means more scrutiny. And for the purpose of building endurance, they were all Erik's in ways he thought necessary.

When training was over she was called to his temporary office. The door locked as it closed and the room shrank.

"You did well, Natalia," Erik said, walking out to meet her.

"Thank you." She was almost happy.

He pushed his thumbs into her shoulders, kneading bone as she undressed and bent over the desk. Through the pendulum of the blinds she saw the dust that colored everything wheat. The bunkers trembling in the sear. The absence of humanity.

"It is a simple assignment. And in a week I'll meet you there." He straightened, zipping up his pants. "Now have you learned your Spanish?"

She laughed. "Where am I going? Mexico?"

"Ask Lucas," he said.

"I don't like that game." She frowned. "Besides, training's over you said."

Out in the world, she was most often Viggo Hjort's wife: when buying guns, guarding the client, making a drop. But for those few last months of 2010, she worked alone in Beirut, becoming familiar with the city, going for long walks by the sea, getting closer to the boy, to the bomb.

The night before the bomb, she startled awake in the dark, queasy with dread. It was only pacing the apartment, drinking Cokes, going over him again and again: Daddy—what he'd looked like, everything he'd ever said—collecting proof that she'd once been a daughter, which allowed Natalia to fall back to sleep. By the time she heard the alarm, her alarm had dissolved; its logic evasive. And by the time she was facing the bathroom mirror brushing her teeth, Erik had arrived in the lobby, and Natalia was ready to be a wife again.

LYNCHBURG, VIRGINIA, 1997

"But I don't wanna go in the kitchen—Bill's still watching TV," Milla said.

Overhead, the fan curdled the air in the trailer and the cicadas beat their bodies against windows that had no screens.

"Go to sleep then." From where she lay on the mattress, Natalia couldn't see the moon, but she could see it pushing bright against the wall.

"My stomach hurts," Milla said.

Natalia yawned. "Put pants on if you're going out there."

Milla flipped onto her back, squeezing up her stomach. "Fat people still get hungry you know. Mom told me I might get skinny when I hit puberty. If I get tall then my fat will stretch out. What? I'm the liar? We were supposed to stop by Bill's then go to Grandma's. I don't know if you've noticed, but this shithole isn't Grandma's."

"Stop moving, you're making the sheet come off. It just got too late to drive."

"You mean Mom got too drunk to drive. If we call Dad—"

"No." Natalia sat up, pointing at her. "You hear me, Milla? No." She flopped back down, fanning her long brown hair across the yellowed pillow. "Besides, it's like a seven-hour time difference."

Milla rolled up. "I'm getting a bowl of cereal."

She grabbed Milla's arm. "Put pants on, I said."

Milla twisted free, making for the kitchen. Natalia scrambled across the mattress, pinning her to the door, hissing, "If you go out there I'll put peanut butter all over your face and set the dog on you."

Milla tried to bite her. Natalia took her by the shoulders and slammed her against the door, smacking her head against the hollow wood, and she dropped to the carpet.

"Hey." Natalia lightly kicked her thigh. "Get up. You're okay." She tried to pull her up by the shoulder. "C'mon. Hey, you're not crying, are you?"

"No." Milla sniffed.

Three years older and a foot taller, Natalia scooped her little sister up.

"Put me down, retard," Milla said.

"Don't say retard." Natalia tossed her onto the mattress. "You're overtired."

Milla rolled away until her forehead touched the wall. "Mom's high."

"She's drunk."

"She got pills from Bill," Milla said. "I saw her."

"She met Bill in rehab."

"I guess she's not cured," said Milla and rolled back to her, watching, waiting, polite.

Natalia sat down. "Already?" She'd had a feeling that this time it would last longer.

Milla pressed her forehead to Natalia's thigh. "What should we do?"

Natalia was still, then she crawled to the foot of the mattress and found Milla's soccer shorts. "Put these on. We're leaving."

"We are?"

Natalia went to the door then turned. "Stay here. I'll be back."

She padded out into the blue sheen of TV. Bill, their mother's new boyfriend, was slack-jawed in the sagging armchair. Maybe a man like him had a gun she might need. She checked the drawers, but in his kitchen thick with trash, she only found his keys. Through the open bedroom door, she could see her mother's feet, something sticky gone black smashed to one heel.

Back in the bedroom, locking the door behind her, she opened the window, hoisting Milla out and lowering her onto the ticking grass.

In the trapped heat of Bill's car, Milla kicked off her sandals, bouncing. "You think you can drive this?"

"I think so," Natalia said, pinching her bottom lip, staring into the now cryptic black of the country road.

"But you've only done parking lots with Daddy."

"When I start it, I'll have to go fast."

"You think they'll call the police on us?"

"They're on drugs," Natalia said, thinking of the gun she didn't have, of ways to get home, of how when their mother picked them up that morning she'd been the mother they couldn't remember but had always wanted. Natalia found the lights and slid in the key. "Seat belt," she said.

THE KALAHARI DESERT, 2002

Why do it to her? Why do it so fast? During her training, Natalia begged him to be patient. To teach her to wait without waiting. "Again?" she asked. "Okay. I'm ready."

God, she was sore. All of inside. She was urine and sweat, but still she longed for water.

Better to be back in the box. Better the water dripping through the cloth over her face. At least then she had her clothes and wasn't spread-eagle on a mattress. "Again?" she asked without ever seeing who she was asking. "Okay, hurry. I'm ready."

When she was little, she always got cold in the ocean. Her lips would turn purple, but still she refused to get out. Because she loved to swim, to feel the force of something bigger all around. "Again?" she asked, or at least made that shape with her mouth.

Erik put a hand on her forehead. "I don't want to hurt you. But this way nobody can."

LEXINGTON, VIRGINIA, 2001

"Well, I'm not gonna pretend this is not the most bullshit thing—" The pause in this tirade was merely in order to wipe a fleck of melting butter from her pearls. Then their mother raised her knife, holding it up like a spear, eyeing both her daughters with something approaching dislike. "Why do you have to be so extreme, girl?" Waiting for no answer, their mother pointed with an oleaginous finger, "You like these? George gave them to me. Aren't they gorgeous?" These pearls were then dangled over Natalia's unmarred hollandaise. "Your father doesn't seem to buy you anything chic so I have no idea what you'd wear them with but they'd sure look pretty on you, honey."

Natalia stared mutely down at three strips of bacon unbroken on her gilt-edged plate, another present from George, who had more money than Bill, than Lon, than even Daddy.

"Talia, I know we're all God's creatures, but can't you at least eat the yoke? It's protein."

"Mom, you know Natalia doesn't eat meat," Milla said.

"But look at those legs—like two strings hanging from your shorts."

"I notice, Mother dearest, that you didn't eat your yoke," said Milla, eating everything but her crusts.

"I'm on a new diet. Now I don't know but I'm not sure those refugees'll have eggs in Kag . . . Kang?"

Natalia looked out the window.

"Kangwa. They'll have eggs," said Milla, unsure.

"Let your sister talk. They won't have chickens cause they're starving for the Lord's sake. Honey. Talia. Look at me, honey. Look at me and not the dead pig."

Milla reached across the table. "I'll eat them."

"Now you don't need them, Milla! Girl, you are getting on my last nerve." Their mother rearranged the bracelets down her arm, spacing them neatly. "Nossir, I am not lending my blessing to this saintly crusade."

"She wants to help people," said Milla, taking the pearls and winding them until they pinched around her wrist.

"She wants to be a martyr," said their mother.

"I believe that qualifies as Jesusy."

"Why don't you just stay here? Didn't you say you'd like

to volunteer at a women's shelter? There's one in Lynchburg. One in Charlottesville too." She elegantly sucked butter off the outside of her palm. "I have a hard time believing that your father of all people thinks this Kang-wah is safe. But then we are speaking of a diplomat that's never successfully brokered a peace. Y'all think he's a saint, but that man only thinks with one of his heads and it doesn't have a cerebral cortex."

Milla spat out her eggs. Natalia frowned at her, saying, "You know it's too early to leave."

"And I want y'all to meet George," said their mother. "He'll be back from work any minute. Look, if you want to travel we could go to Paris. Would you like that? That's where George took me on our honeymoon. Just like Lon and your daddy. Talia, make eye contact. People are gonna take you for an Asperger's. I am certain they got people in need in France."

"A Saturday and he's at work?" Milla said. "Have you ever wondered if he's having an affair? With his intern mayhaps? I'm not saying for definite, but you'd be stupid to rule it out. I mean, Exhibit A, Dad."

Natalia pushed away from the table and stood. "You win. I'm calling us a cab."

On the train from Charlottesville to D.C., Milla picked her cuticles bloody. "I have decided to pawn Mom's pearls. Yo quiero un new bike. How much do you think I'll get?"

"We were supposed to take the three P.M. It's only eleven. Now Daddy's going to want to know why we're home early."

"He shouldn't have made us come," Milla said.

"It's her birthday." Natalia took their tickets from her backpack. "I guess I'll tell him I felt sick."

"Are you proposing you lie? Thou? What kind of dastardly—"

"Did you steal her Valium?" asked Natalia.

Milla held up a vial. "You perhaps refer to this? Did thou not witnesseth that they give her the shakes? I call it an act of grace."

"What do they do to you?" Natalia tried to grab it.

"Fuck off." Milla sat on the vial. "They make my scalp hot. Occasionally. If Mom does any more she's gonna be in eternal pause."

"Let me look at your hands. They're bleeding. Milla, fine, I'm not going to take it."

Milla held out her hands and Natalia wiped them off with the underside of her T-shirt.

"Maybe you'll save some hot refugee's soul."

Natalia showed the passing train conductor their tickets. "They're already Christian, dumbass."

"But are they Faith Redeemers we ask ourselves?"

"Ask the pastor," said Natalia.

"I don't talk to that wolf in sheep's clothing, that charlatan, that—"

"—Machiavel?" Natalia finished.

"I hope you know," said Milla, "that I'm not ever going to Mom's without you. She'll have to wait till you come back."

"It's only for a year." Natalia leaned back against the hum of her seat, watching a tattoo of waves rippling around the bicep of a man in a bleached tank top weaving down the aisle, steadying himself on the headrests. "Maybe she'll be sober when I get back."

"I've never told you don't go, did I? Nope, because I'm not like her. *I* would never do that. You sure you don't want these?" asked Milla, whipping the pearls in Natalia's face.

"Stop."

"If you don't want them I'm going to go between the train cars and throw them out. Because I don't want them. Unless you want them?"

"Stop, Milla."

"Do you want them?"

"Get out of my face." Natalia snatched the pearls from Milla.

"See, you wanted them."

WASHINGTON, D.C., 2001

The morning she was leaving for Kangwa, Daddy made her milk drowned over sugared coffee. It was in the dining room, before the sun before the airport before the refugee camp before the massacre before she was kidnapped recruited trained before she knew snipers before she knew checkpoints, Daddy lifted the heat-heavy hair off her forehead and asked if she was ready saying We aren't going to wait because Milla is not coming down to say good-bye.

GUANAJUATO, 2005

In a night of steam, Natalia walked into the grim cantina and bought a Coke. Outside, dust swept over the road and the people were slick with heat. Her tank top, already sticking to her back, sagged under the haze of the cantina's red and teal Christmas lights. She counted five men inside. They had a careless menace.

Erik was sitting at a sodden bar wide enough for three. In Copenhagen, he'd been in a tux, but here he was dressed in a

T-shirt and khaki shorts stained above the knees. His blond hair was long and he'd grown a thick beard. He had come as Christien.

She walked by him, choosing one of the plastic tables facing the entrance and smoothing down her short hair. Immediately, he swaggered over with two tequilas.

"May I join you?" His blue eyes had gone small in the lean red bloat of his face.

"Of course, yes," she said in Spanish.

"What is your name?"

"Anastasia, but everybody calls me Ana."

They drank—the smell of meat frying on their skin—until the cantina emptied to the bartender and waitress. Uneasy, she'd been careful to pour most of the tequilas under the table and into the dark.

"Why don't you come here." He patted his lap.

She sat on him and he tipped her chin, looking into her eyes. "You must remain Ana."

It was her first assignment alone. She had been living in a seedy hotel for days, constipated and unable to eat. Mosquitoes preyed on her, waking her every hour because she slept with the light on.

"I am," she said, annoyed. From over his shoulder, she saw the bartender looking at her, a different bartender, she thought, than the one before.

"Ana is not Natalia. Cut contact with Arturo."

She liked Arturo. "Okay."

"Two blocks west is your new hotel. Room eleven. There is a key in your pocket. A nine-millimeter under the mattress. Do not leave the room until you hear from Victor."

"Who's Victor? It's raining."

"Your new source. Arturo is dead. You will have to run or get soaked."

"What happened?" she asked though the death was as distant to her as if it had been committed centuries ago.

"He was beheaded," Erik said. He looked like he hadn't slept either. "You see why I tell you that you must be careful to remain Ana?"

Arturo had said he had a girlfriend who was pregnant. "Was it the cartel?" Now the baby had no father. "Who told them he was talking to us?" She swallowed a mouthful of tequila.

He shook his head, dismissive. "We will deal with them later. Give it no thought. Concentrate on the task at hand."

But she was trying to remember Arturo's girlfriend's name. Luz? Liliana? It was a name she liked. The waitress was watching her.

He tilted back in his chair and lit a cigarette. "It's getting late. You're lingering."

But like a child from its mother, she didn't want to be parted.

"Don't worry," he said. "I'm never far."

"Why are you Christien?" she whispered into her tequila.

Erik's laugh was coarse, amplified, detached.

"Mitt hjärta,"—two fingers traced Natalia's spine—"he's the one who puts them on the rack."

BEIRUT, 2011

Natalia was nothing but a faceless body of about medium height stumbling toward the agents through the ruins of drooping concrete. A bad fit in a men's oversized sweatshirt. Blood browning where there might have been a nose.

When the hood was removed and the hair from her eyes and the gag from her mouth, she produced a smile, which revealed that either in the explosion, or perhaps during the beatings, she had lost more than one tooth.

"Natalia Edwards?" asked the suit guiding her into the backseat.

She hesitated then nodded, her eyes watering. It had been so long since she'd heard an American accent; it sounded like a banjo. The driver was older, anonymous, monitoring both her and the road. The agent was young and sandy-haired, his scalp showing pink through his hair's part.

He handed her a bottle of water and the van began to move away, perhaps toward the embassy. She closed her eyes, feeling him looking. She felt no real interest in the agent, even if he was saving her from the blandly unbearable pain of the police.

"Does my family know I'm alive?" she asked.

"The State Department has contacted your father," he said. "Are you cold? We've got blankets in the back."

She drank more water, swishing it around, tasting the dank iron of old blood, trying not to ask about Erik. "Is he coming to get me?"

"Well, that's a little complicated, isn't it, Ms. Edwards? Since you and your fellow consultants have been interfering with military operations."

She turned back to the window, hiding her face, seeing what the sun had bleached.

"So of course," the agent hurried on, "we have a few questions, before you see him, before we can let you back in the States, before—"

"—Before I get medical attention," Natalia finished without turning.

She dropped the emptied water bottle. It rolled into the tip of the agent's loafer. He gave a waspish, mechanical smile like an actor in a bad play.

PRESENT, WASHINGTON, D.C.

In the black-and-white picture, Daddy is squatting in the grass at the bottom of a green hill that photographed gray. His left arm is reaching to pet a monstrous cat. It is an unwanted advance. The sun has whited out his left side. Wite-Out, as in the corrective product, the pungent neon white paste that obscures but does not hide a mistake, and white out, the meteorological phenomenon where due to snow or sand the horizon is erased, no shadows are cast and one is blinded by white. Both of these are in effect.

In the future, depending on what artifacts remain, people might suppose him a saint, blessing the cat, absolving it of its sins in contrast to the grubby schoolgirl on his right, whose hand, also outstretched, is about to yank the cat's head.

In this picture, Milla is little again. Her smile has more than a couple of gaps. She has a boy's haircut: heavy bangs and shaved at the neck. The right side of her face, the side farthest away from Daddy, is in shadow.

Natalia's not in it. But somehow she's there. You just can't see her.

BEIRUT, 2011

"Any other names, aliases?"

(Katya Durmashkina, Anastasia Ray, Lynn Feldman, Suheir Ali.)

"Do I need to repeat that?"

"Lawyer." Natalia sat blindfolded and strapped to a chair.

"I apologize but I don't think there's any in town. Why were you tailing the boy? You might as well speak freely at this point. Your CEO, Erik Carlsson"—she heard the agent flipping through a file—"alias Viggo Hjort, Nils Tjader, Lucas Westerberg, Christien Thomsen, died in the explosion. Risk Control International has closed."

"There he is," Erik had said in her ear.

"Are you sure?" she'd asked.

"Of course," he said. "Do it before he gets any closer to the building. Are you ready?"

Her neck ached as she'd leaned forward through the blown-out window. There was a place in her neck where she carried the day they'd met. A knot which sometimes slid to her shoulder. A hard, desert pain that would not be pushed out.

"Now," her husband said.

All she had to do was shoot the boy with a bomb strapped to his back, the boy in the suicide vest. But she had not expected him to be beautiful. To be seventeen with God on his lips.

She went backward out of the room, down the stairs, through the front door until she was facing where the boy stood on the other side of the street. Through the traffic, the boy saw her, his eyes the color of the sea.

As she saw him going for the detonator, the dust bit and bled her ears. The scorched graffiti of the pocked buildings was eaten invisible. She'd crawled over a child's bike and into a red arc of blood. The arm chewed off by the blast was not the boy's, and she checked, not hers. She tried to radio Erik. Shouting his every name, and since no one could hear, the name for the father she'd once had.

The heavy steel door opened and a soldier stepped into the interrogation room. "Sir? We have a situation."

The agent stood, scraping his chair back.

The door closed. Her forehead dropped to the table. Erik gone. Her husband. Her boss. Her man.

The door opened. She sat up. Katya's hands folded in Ana's lap; Suheir crying under her blindfold; Lynn's burns starting to itch. She heard arguing.

"Daddy," she said.

PRESENT, WASHINGTON, D.C.

The bed is too comfortable. She's stripped the sheets. How can she sleep in this room where soccer shrines hang with the blue ribbons of state championships? Where a poster of Milla with her foot on the ball is signed at the bottom in black marker? Where her sister's high school reading list lines the book shelf? Where all the objects of Milla are intact except the plastic white stars lining the ceiling that no longer light up when Natalia plugs them in? She is the wrong sister in the wrong room, the daughter who died but is still alive.

Natalia leaves Milla's room and goes downstairs where the house is buzzing with Daddy's high-tech security alarm, the radioactive locusts and AC. She opens a Coke and lays on the couch with the lights out. She can feel the ghost of Milla stomping down the hall, affectionate and graceless, going into the kitchen to make brownies. Her own room has been made into a study.

The wind picks up and she hears the trees beating each other in the backyard. She gets up and peers at the photographs on the wall, finding one of her high school graduation, a shiny girl in a shiny blue gown—vice president, Key Club, National Honor Society—she'd played soccer too but was never as good.

She picks up her Coke and turns off the AC. If she could just see Milla for five minutes and put her arms around her, tell her she loves her. But Milla won't come to the house or answer her calls. She doesn't forgive her for not coming back, for letting them think she was dead, for failing to be the good, big sister. They'll never be close again because of all she did and did not do.

In the kitchen, his chair turned to the sliding glass doors, Daddy sits in an old robe waiting for morning. Natalia can feel the tiredness radiate off him. In Beirut, when she first saw him, she could feel she was his daughter, felt the lines of their lives intersect. But now that she's home, they're strangers, afraid of blaming each other, then hating each other, and losing each other all over again.

"Hey, honey." He looks older than sixty in the hangdog of his neck and chin. She's aged him. "Have some of our fine Colombian coffee. Did you get any sleep on that old couch?"

"Not much." Natalia hesitates, then pulls up a chair next to him like she used to in the mornings before school. "Are you going back to Bogotá?"

"Not for a while yet." He crosses an ankle over his knee. "I have to go into the office and throw my weight around while they're investigating you."

"I hope it won't affect your position."

"I'm almost retired." He puts a hand on the top of her head. It stays there for an impossible moment, then unable to stand it, she gets up and goes to the counter.

"This one looks familiar," she says, facing the cupboard and taking down a mug. "Turkey Trot." She looks back at him. "Daddy?"

He's watching the birds outside. "You came in fifth."

"Daddy. I don't want you to think I'm ungrateful."

"I'd call you lucky," he says, not without bitterness.

"Somehow I don't feel very lucky." She puts the mug back and chooses another. "Look . . . I can't live here, I can't stay in Milla's old room. It doesn't feel right."

"I'll arrange something," he says slowly, his eyes on a red cardinal.

"Don't worry about me, I'll take care of it."

He looks at her. "I'm on the line for you, Natalia. If you want to stay elsewhere, then we're talking a place of my choosing." He looks back out the window. In the backyard, the sun is tearing the horizon pink. "And I'd like you to see your mother before you go." He uncrosses his legs. "There's cream in the fridge."

"Sugar?"

"By the stove. At least there's one thing about you that hasn't changed." He waits. "Do I still know you?"

It's the question she's been dreading. "I don't know," she says.

"Your mother has not changed. But when we thought you were gone, Milla needed her and so I finally had to give over to God and forgive the woman."

"I don't expect forgiveness."

He gets up. "Well you make it so damn hard. You're only home because that man is dead—" He cuts himself off, oddly out of breath.

But she can't speak to her father of Erik. It seems a violation to mention him. Instead she says, "You said you have a heart condition? What does that mean?"

"They scraped out my arteries. Give me another." He holds out his mug and she pours in fresh coffee. Then he rests the mug on his knee, watching the liquid slant then settle. "Didn't I teach you to value your family and your faith?"

"Am I on trial?"

"Not before me, but when the time comes I worry for your soul," he says.

She wants to tell him that she couldn't shoot the boy because of him, couldn't take one life to keep a hundred, couldn't save Erik because he taught her to fear the stain on her immortal soul.

"I thought you had to die to the world to save it." She looks into his tired red eyes. "I was wrong."

KANGWA, 2001

After the women's prayer group, Natalia left the confines of the tents—tarps stretched over a patchwork of corrugated tin. She walked along the outside of the camp, looking out at the border: a bronzed, anonymous nineteen-year-old girl. Near a pile of plastic debris and broken cooking pots, there was a Humvee.

"Hello," said the driver in English. He was a giant blond man. Under his American accent, there was a foreign undulation.

"Hello," she said, apprehensive, looking around for any other person.

"You shouldn't be out here alone." He had pale, sad eyes that looked like they were being drained. "The local patrolmen aren't above rape. You are part of the Faith Redeemed Ministry?"

"Yes sir, we're building an orphanage." She wondered who he was. Not old, not young, remote but not condescending.

"I thought that all of you had returned to the States," he said.

"Some of us are staying with our pastor."

"Has he mentioned that the army is heading east? They're looking for Rebels hiding in these camps."

She shrugged. "This camp is just widows and kids."

"You should leave," he said without urgency.

"We want to finish what we've started," she said, repeating the words her pastor had said that morning.

"What about your family?" he asked. "Don't they think you should be coming home?"

"I'm nineteen."

"I see," he said, smiling and leaning out of the window. "I am Erik."

She relaxed under his smile. "Natalia. Are you German?"

"Swedish. I like the name Natalia. It becomes you."

When he said her name, it was as if he saw only her and the rest of the world blurred behind her. Then she felt ugly in her stained tie-dye T-shirt, her worn Tevas, the gold cross necklace from Daddy. "I should get back," she said, gesturing weakly at the camp. "They're expecting me."

Natalia woke with the screaming. She lay for too long sweating under her wool blanket. The shots seemed to be coming from the opposite side of the camp.

She crawled out of her tent and found people pushing in every direction. She rushed to the pastor's tent, but it was on fire. Stepping back, she turned into a pile of men's bodies, some facedown, some spilled at odd angles, all of them curled and flailed against one another, and next to them was a heap of children lying like discarded toys, legs burned, their small heads full of bloody gaps. She screamed, but no one seemed to know her. Only a young soldier came toward her, dragging a woman already gouged by bullets and she ran—running toward the blue line of morning as if eventually she would become it. For it seemed to her that there was only the earth and no God.

Natalia was at the edge of the camp, lying next to an old woman with a mouthful of flies. A man was speaking over her in a language she did not understand. He was wearing fatigues and handed another man his gun, then carried her body to a truck bed. Over the scalding metal, she stared up at a placid sky. She knew then that she had died.

Erik held a canteen to her peeling lips and cupped the back of her head. He put a jacket over her waist, saying in English, "You're in shock." He opened a medical kit. "This will sting," he said. Her eyes closed. His hum was louder than thought. Then he was gone, and she too went.

Then Erik said, "Open your legs," not knowing that she was only a body.

There was another man standing with him, bearded, uneager.

"He has been trained as a doctor. He must look."

The man said something. He looked even more harassed. Her body jerked when he touched her knee, causing the jacket to slip. There was dried blood on her thighs.

"Breathe," Erik said, holding her shoulders to the truck bed.

Someone somewhere was making a terrible sound.

Erik pressed the jacket over her mouth. "It will all be over soon." He peeled one of her hands from the side of the truck and held it.

Her foot kicked then her body dropped back. Tears wet the sides of her hair. Her legs parted.

"Söt flicka." He smoothed the tears. "Let us take care of you."

After he and the man had spoken, she was propped against Erik in the truck bed, her head under his chin.

"We couldn't interfere," he said, his fingers combing out the clots of dirt in her hair. "It isn't what we were hired to do—it's against the interest of the mining company allied with the army."

"I don't understand . . . Are you a soldier?" Her lips split when she spoke.

"A mercenary," he said. "And they"—he gestured at a truck behind them beginning to pull away—"they are a private military. They're leaving before the UN arrive. I've finished my contract and will stay with you until they come. But you must call me Viggo."

"Why?"

"Because Erik has a criminal record, while Viggo is an accountant."

She closed her eyes. "Is everyone I knew dead?"

"Some escaped. You'll find them and go back to the States."

She thought of her childhood bedroom, of Milla, of Daddy, of the mundane safety of home and was repelled. "I can't," she said.

"Why not?"

"Because somewhere on the other side of the world I'm screaming."

He was silent for a moment, then said, "What happened to you was a short hell."

She opened her eyes. "Where will you go?"

"Back to Stockholm. I'm opening my own company. Not a little army but a group of analysts."

She wet her cracked lips. "Do you know what the soldiers did to me?"

"I know," he said.

She shifted in his arms, hugging herself. "Do you know exactly?"

"I can make a very good guess."

"Because you're a mercenary," she said then reached up, stopping his hand in her hair. "Have you done what they did?"

"No." He brought her hand down and held it. "But not one of us is better than any other."

She turned to see his face. From that angle, he looked like a minor god who knows the world but is not of it.

"You're safe, young, and alive," he said. "The only thing that matters is now. Say it over and over."

"I wish I was like you," she said, looking into the wreckage of the tents and though she was dead she tried to breathe.

THE KALAHARI DESERT, 2002

"What are you thinking of?" he asked.

"Sleep. Bacon," she said.

"You need to center yourself. Find a focal point."

"How can I if I can't see?"

"Begin to feel your feet spreading on the ground. Empty your body. You must remember this when you're frightened and know that terrible things are about to be done."

"Should I be frightened?"

"Let go of thought, let go of your body."

When he carried the heat of her in his arms, Natalia knew safety. She knew that if she could be with Erik, she would not fear death. If they would not be parted, death would be okay, whatever the eternal boredom, possible nothingness, lack of personality. If she could be with Erik, death would take only her body.

"Are you there?" she asked.

"I'm here," Viggo said.

"Again?" she asked.

"I'm coming in," Nils said.

"Who?" she asked.

"Again," Lucas said. "Almost over," said Christien and Natalia was cold.

"Erik?" she asked.

"Yes," he said.

"I'm ready."

The Peculiar Narrative of the Remarkable Particulars in the Life of Orrinda Thomas,

AN AMERICAN SLAVE

WRITTEN BY HERSELF.

"THE POETRY OF THE EARTH IS NEVER DEAD"

~ KEATS

PUBLISHED BY ASHWELL & CRAWFORD,

STATIONERS' HALL COURT

1840

EDITOR'S NOTE

Upon the Editor's journeying south to Turnwood Plantation in order to discover what fate had befallen his younger brother, Frederick Crawford, he was acquainted with these papers whose tale furnishes that history. At the time of its composition, its author,

Orrinda Thomas, who has been known to the Editor since a child, could not foresee what barbarous events would transpire. Yet the Editor can attest that he has found these eloquent words to be not only written unaided, but deplorably true, and a rebuke to those who revel in the oppression of their fellow man and dare to do it in Christ Jesus's name. It is the Editor's intention to demonstrate how the pernicious cruelty and terror of slavery in this country endangers all men black and white, from North to South.

RALPH CRAWFORD
BOSTON, March 25th, 1840

———

August 28th, 1838

We sleep outside so we will not be smothered. The breeze rolls in from the river, over the levee, down the corridor of oak trees and into our makeshift bedrooms on the verandah. It is late August, and Louisiana is the eighth circle of Hell.

Last night, I watched the smoke from the sugar vats. Observed that the Spanish moss in my mattress is hardly flat. (Likely the house slaves do not think mine worthy of the rolling pin.) I could not sleep for waiting. For what? Keats's immortal Nightingale? The Communion of William Cullen Bryant? Nothing in the wind but night and smoke. Yet, near dawn, my reward:

Lord, You alone have chosen me, yet
this ornate darkness keeps me from sleep.

The lines came with that queer, molten flush
which signals a passion of Poesy. But instead of the
customary frenzy of the next passage, I was seized by
the unnerving certainty that one day Greatness shall
indeed be conferred upon me, and I will be more than
the High Brown Bard, the Sable Songstress, the Nigger
Muse . . . and simply Orrinda Thomas, poet. The price
of the Sublime remains to be seen.

Your superstition is getting worse with age, said
Crawford buttering his toast this morning as we sat
in Turnwood's rose and ivory dining room, the gold-
framed figures of the plantation's patriarchs sternly
disgusted by the sight of a black woman sharing *le petit
dejeuner* with a white man.

"Think of Orpheus," I said.

"Jam?" he asked.

"No, I thank you—whose song moved Gods and
mortals alike. Despite his greatness, Orpheus was torn
to pieces by the Maenads. They could not hear his voice
for their howls."

"Your thesis?" he asked, stirring his tea.

"It is the poet's Bad End," I said, lifting my cup.

But this foreboding is not solely my fancy. Our
arrival in Louisiana did not augur well. On our way to
Turnwood Plantation, our carriage stopped at a town
but I did not descend. It was as if everything bad that
ever happened there had lingered. Goodness did not live

there, only a suspicious poverty of the Spirit. Porches
offered barefoot children aged in their movements, and
men whose eyes repeated the violence done to them.

Crawford climbed down from our carriage, leading
the horses to a trough of water (outside of what we
took to be their General Store—more resembling an
outhouse). He tipped his hat to the clerk with his
unrelenting air of refinement, but that fellow was too
busy gaping at me to notice Crawford hiss through his
teeth: "Orrinda, do not get down." The children had
begun drifting toward us like white gnats.

When I was a child, I developed the infernal,
nervous habit of smiling when about to get a beating.
I'd be begging hard for forgiveness all the while
grinning. Mrs. Johnson would be winded trying
to thrash the smile out of me, so what had I to do
yesterday morning but sit in the carriage and Smile?

Crawford tossed his top hat in the carriage and leapt
up, shouting to the horses as the children clotted and
swarmed, throwing eggs and rocks, howling oaths at
our backs. (Baboon and the like.) Somehow they had
gotten wind that the Savage Poet had come.

"This journey is foolish beyond permission!" I cried,
hugging my head to my knees.

"The more fool you for consenting to come with
me!" Crawford laughed, lashing the horses on.

"But why in the world do we skip gaily into the
belly of the beast?" I wailed. "It is one thing for me to
be a learned Negro in Boston, but Louisiana?"

"O Orrinda . . ." Thankfully, he was struck in the

neck by an egg. The yoke of indignity silenced his ill-considered oratory until we slid into the haze of the pines; the town clinging like an illness just past which leaves one sour and weak.

At last, Crawford slackened the reins, saying, "We should see this as proof of how mightily you are needed here."

"Oh yes," I said, smoothing out my skirt. "They need me hanging from one of these trees."

"Come now. We must be brave. Do you not see that of all the places that must witness Negroes not as beasts of burden but as brethren capable of Beauty. Bards—"

"Being bludgeoned by alliteration! I do hope that isn't the new Introduction to my book, Crawford."

"Minx," he said, rubbing his neck with his handkerchief. "Is the egg gone? This is a new cravat."

"But truly, if I am not greatly mistaken these Southerners have no wish to see me as any thing more than a nigger parrot who has forgotten her cage. I've never performed farther South than Philadelphia, I fear—"

"Look." Crawford drew the carriage to a halt. "Perfectly haunting," he said.

I looked. The trees tunneled over us, grim and decadent, dark in their green. I wondered what terrified fugitives lurked in the marshes.

"Won't you please," he begged.

As is by far his worst habit, Crawford likes me to recite whenever we flee a mob. I leaned back in my seat, tipping my face to the threatening trees:

My Love is deeper than my Desire
To possess. It is a living thing
That doth remain though I expire
To bed the field and turn the page. It sings
Past me, voice an opiate choir.
'Tis more than the love I desire.

Crawford gaily applauded my poem, the prospect of those we shall conquer, and the money we will receive because of it. I only hope I live to again see the East.

Last night, I heard the bell of my girlhood. I began to perspire the lonely revulsion of Virginia, a state sixteen years past. Like one possessed, I left my bed on the Turnwood verandah and drifted along the balustrade to the back of the Great House. From the second-floor window, I saw the slaves coming up through the dark, passing the overseer, his hand itching on a whip of cowhide, and watched them fill their empty gourds in the trough and disappear into the waving cane. By dawn, the fields were burning with song.

Dinnertime now. How on earth will I eat while being served by them? Will read before bed. Am but twenty pages into Mary Shelley's *Mathilda*. Though already it is darkly—indeed lavishly sentimental, I am again persuaded by Crawford's taste in the Gothic. Perhaps I should try my hand at the Novel?

Yours, &c.
Orrinda

August 29th, 1838

This morning Crawford insisted we ride to the
slave market in New Orleans. To be brief, I told him I
would rather sit in the stocks. To which he replied: "My
dear, I should deserve only your trust." I could hardly
persuade my legs to the door. Crawford was Very
Much Disappointed in my Lack of Spirit and remained
Certain Fine Poetry Shall Come of It. The man is
torturous for my Art. I cannot agree with this punitive
bent of Philosophy, though I have ever regarded it as
a Truth that Pain can yield worthy literary Sentiment,
but can it not also give way to the utter tripe of the
Sentimental?

Yet as I am but a toy, a jade in a cage, a darling
spectacle, I went.

I will confess that since arriving to the Inferno di
Turnwood, I am not myself. Though I am treated here
in the grand style, my mind misgives. The Widow
Turnwood's gestures are falsely sugared. Ha. And for
what purpose? I cannot fancy why the owner of at least
thirty slaves would pay *me* twenty hundred dollars
merely to recite?? And there is something more . . .
nagging . . . like the spectre behind these the moon-
fretted trees: tender and indignant.

And my Crawford. . . . Do I condemn his avidity,
which has led me to Turnwood, or do I commend
his mad heart, which has, in the liveliest sympathy,
liberated me?

Crawford feels we can convert the Widow to the
Great Cause. *Malo periculosam, libertatem quam*

quietam servitutem. But I find in her no Angelina Grimké. If the Widow Turnwood's conscience is so troubled, why not set her slaves free, or simply leave? Crawford says she has been a widow but a year, is convent-raised, and claims to have been kept up till now utterly apart from the pernicious workings of Turnwood.

Before we left for the slave market, the Widow, not knowing whither we were bound, requested my presence in the parlor for the first time since our arrival. I went upstairs and told Crawford, who gave a Solomon grin, saying: "Her timing is impeccable."

I followed him down the stairs onto the second-floor landing. "Cannot you tell it?" I said. "I am much too fatigued."

He stopped. "But it is you who are her curio." He lifted my curls from my shoulders, turning me to arrange them down my back.

"But I believe *you've* inspired some tender emotions in that lily-white heart."

"Perhaps." He smiled. "I was a bit too forward in our correspondence."

"If by that you mean you encouraged her to harbor romant—"

"I mean," he interrupted, "I got her up to twenty hundred dollars." He twisted my hair into a chignon. "My sweet girl, you are too cruel. Think upon the money. Shall we wear it up for the reading? A confection of piety and exposure?" He tucked his chin over my right shoulder. "You shan't have to tour for a

year if you don't wish. You will have time to compose.
Is this not what you wanted?"

"I would rather do a hundred performances in
Massachusetts than one here," I said. "This place
exhausts me, it is a reproof to see their wounds, hear
their cries while I mince about free."

"But if this venture is a success—"

"Then what?" I stepped away. "Who knows how
many other disconsolate, rich widows secluded in
palmetto-fringed oases of bondage would wish to
witness the circus of my verse?"

"Why limit ourselves to a Northern audience?" he
asked.

"I do not imagine the Widow knows the difference
between Byron and Mrs. Sigourney!"

"Remember to touch your collarbone," he said.
"It—"

"Signals fragility. I know!"

He held out his hand. And because . . . O I know not
what excuse to give but I took it.

"I adore you," he said.

We walked down the curling staircase along a
painted fresco and into the foyer until we stood outside
the parlor door.

"I know that too," I said, letting go of his hand.
"Endeavor to come in on your cue, won't you?"

How to describe Madam Sop? She is a fair, willowy,
round-faced creature. Moon-faced, I would say. This
is not to suggest she is not prettyish what with her

streaming golden hair and cornflower blue eyes (a poor man's Lady Rowena) but that her countenance is marred by her perpetually startled expression. She droops like a guilty puppet; head too big for her body. Her manner appears one of cloying docility but her nails are bitten to the quick. In short, she is a pitiable creature so why do I despise her? *Why?* For she is the sort of Southerner who loves to hear the colored man sing his sorrows but would never forgo the ease of her daily luxuries to not be the origin of his lament.

In the oppressive mahogany of the gilt crimson parlor, we sat in the clock-notched silence until the Widow Turnwood gathered the audacity necessary for speech, uttering: "Thank you for doing me the honor of coming to Turnwood."

"Indeed no, it is I, ma'am, who must thank you for your gracious and bold invitation," I said.

She inhaled sharply, "Will you read 'I Walked in Cambridge'?"

"Whatever you wish," I simpered.

She gazed into the black marble fireplace. "I wonder if I could ask you . . ."

"Please, ask me any thing at all. For you, I am an open book."

"How is it that Mr. Crawford discovered you?"

Curtain up. The harmless, belaurel'd Negro takes center stage. I cleared my throat and took a sip of tea: "I was born in Virginia to Mr. William Thomas. He had a plantation some twenty miles from Manassas. My father was Mr. Thomas's brother. My mother had once belonged to Mr. Thomas, but shortly after my birth was sold to a nearby farm. Her name was Delia. I was Mr. Thomas's daughter's slave. Though dear Belinda was more like a sister to me."

"Do you recall your mother?" the Widow asked.

"Some Sundays she would get a pass and come up to the Great House while the other slaves were congregating for their weekly serving of flour and lard, but my image of her is dim. Every year I imagine a different face . . ." I've always hated that line. I am fully sensible of its truth but how long it has been since I experienced it as true!

Crawford burst into the parlor: "Orrinda, I hope—" Then, feigning affectionate surprise: "Mrs. Turnwood? Oh, why good morning! Had I known you were present, I never would have so carelessly interrupted. I beg your pardon."

A premature entrance overdone. Wasted on the Widow. For him, she is already captive.

"I was telling her of Belinda," I said.

"Dear Belinda," Crawford cried, "whose unpolluted kindness we shall not soon forget! It is she who taught Orrinda to read and write and speak French."

"Yes," I agreed flatly. "I was a happy child then for I scarcely comprehended I was a slave."

"But what happened to her?" asked the Widow.

I stared fixedly into a supposedly unfathomable distance. "One day, Belinda turned blue. Her little neck swelled like a bull's, and she died." I swallowed an imagined lump. "After the death of her child, Mrs. Thomas fast followed, and Mr. Thomas quitted the plantation, sending his slaves to the speculator."

Here, Crawford dropped his head and voice in a compassionate brood and thus began to pace: "Orrinda was made to march for miles to the auction block. Her bare feet bloody, ankles raw from chains. When finally they reached their destination, the stench of the pens was that of human misery. There, rubbed with bacon fat to appear healthy, Orrinda was bought by Mr. Johnson of Southern Virginia. Then one afternoon, when she was but eleven years old, she was sent into the parlor with a tray of refreshments for Miss Julia, Mr. Johnson's daughter, and Miss Julia's Northern guests."

"I was not in good spirits." I smiled tremulously. "For old Mrs. Johnson had seen me spill molasses and tied me to a tree, stripping me from head to waist and whipping me until she was defeated by her own fatigue."

"Orrinda had no kin," murmured Crawford, coming to stand behind my chair. "No Belinda, no mammy to grease her torn back so her dress would not stick. She slept alone in the corner of the attic on a pile of rags. Awake half the night with hunger. But as Orrinda set the tray on the table, Miss Julia, fresh from Lady's Seminary, began to read from a slim volume."

"I could not know then," I said rising valiantly to my feet. "That it was 'The Lake' by Alphonse de Lamartine. I knew only of a provoking familiarity and stopped, rapt, deciphering. *L'homme n'a point de port, le temps n'a point de rive; il coule, et nous passons.* I did not realize that I had been thus standing, when a gentleman of about medium height stepped from the visitors and remarked upon it."

"It was Mr. Crawford!" breathed the Widow, clasping both her hands together.

"Yes!" I trilled. "Who is this? he asked Miss Julia. Why that is little Orrinda, Miss Julia said. Do you know French, Orrinda? he asked. Miss Julia laughed, Don't be absurd, Frederick—what a notion! But he said, *Connaissez-vous français?* I could not help but answer him: *Oui monsieur je fais. Ai-je eu des ennuis? Où suis-je pas?* Miss Julia, shocked into indignation, ordered me out. But instead of going into the kitchen to grate corn, I hid upstairs in the linen closet. The next morning, when finally my belly overcame my fear, I emerged. But instead of a whipping, I was told to wash, for the gentleman who had spoken French had bought me and would be my deliverer."

"How peculiar," murmured the Widow.

Yet I think that Chapter is the least peculiar of all. What of that day we first set out for Boston? Being overawed by this man, differing so widely from any of the men of my acquaintance, I was made mute. I had no very clear notion of what would be expected of me, neither did I know that I now belonged to a Northern man who had no house, no farm, nor any other slaves. The second son of a large Unitarian family, Crawford was intended for Divinity, then perhaps Law, but had instead left Harvard to roam the country.

That night he gave me the corn bread in his saddlebag while he kindled a fire. I stayed by the horse, a creature I understood.

When he sat down to warm himself, he laughed. "I'm not going to eat you, child."

He has a high, inelegant laugh that makes his eyes slit.

"Wouldn't you like to sit?" he suggested.

I squat down on the other side of the fire, all agitation; the corn bread molding to my fist.

"You are perhaps wondering why I bought you," he began. "I admit I am also wondering this myself. But when you stood there, Orrinda, so transported, and answered me in French—French! A single phrase entered my mind: *By grace ye are saved.* And I knew I had to save you, you poor wretch. I saw that barbarous old witch, Mrs. Johnson, giving you a whipping out by the barn, mutilating your little back."

I uncurled the corn bread and began to love him.

He closed his eyes and leaned back against a tree. "You know, I saw Buckminster in the pulpit once. I was only a boy, but after seeing his performance I knew I could resign my ecclesiastical ambitions. My family was mistaken in me. You see, I've always had grace, but in Boston, they want holy novelty." He looked at me with eyes cavalier, gray, and acute. "And wouldn't they flock"—he smiled— "to hear you recite unimpeachable French."

Thus ended my days as a slave.

Today in the slave market no muse arrived. Only we appeared amid the throng in the form of two subdued visitors. How could we become contemplative when Cato's back made so great an impression? It was skin made drought, ridged with the memory of fish.

I wish God would see fit to tell me why Cato's

life should have been one of undeserved torture and I should escape. What am I that I do not suffer like him? In the pens, I saw manacled babes destined to be parted without mercy from their mothers whose lives will descend into insupportable grief. I could not stand there idle, well fed in silk.

I leaned forward and squeezed Crawford's arm. "Do you see him?"

"Who?"

"The one they're about to bid for. Look at him. Bid."

Crawford peered round a portly man to glimpse the block. "For that poor, blistered devil? I don't know that Mrs. Turnwood would appreciate the gift."

"Not for her."

He looked at me. "Are you mad? We are here to witness this earthly hell, no more—we're bound to see a thousand wretches like him."

"He'll go for nothing. I'll pay for him from my earnings."

"Orrinda, if we dare free this man, Turnwood's neighbors will string us up before you've spoken a single stanza," he said.

The bidding for Cato began, but no buyers lingered, for the marks were to them a sure sign of rebellion.

"Did you not say that in Louisiana I would be a beacon in this darkest hour of inhumanity?" I hissed.

"We are not here to seek confrontation—not to mention how we are grossly outnumbered! We endeavor to enlighten as we entertain."

I looked at my Crawford. There is as of yet no white in his hair, but it has begun its peaked retreat and the skin around his eyes is lined and thin. Though his eyes are those same waves in winter and around their dark centers, gold blooms. I have memorized this face and know its every crease, stray whisker, secret expression.

"I believe you claimed to adore me? Then buy him," I said.

Crawford pinched and slapped Cato's arms and thighs. Made a show of inspecting his teeth. Then strutted to the back of the market to strip Cato naked and pay $400 for him.

In the carriage, waiting for Crawford to obtain the Bill of Sale, Cato examined me, noting my fine dress, store-bought shoes, and unabashed familiarity with his new master. Gaunt and dusty, his perturbed eyes fairly bent from his face. All I could do was smile and offer water. In such a hostile crowd, I dared not tell him he was to be freed.

He hesitated and with a hunted look asked, "Miss, he a fair marster?"

"Very fair," I said.

"Because I'se belonged to the meanest white man that ever walked the earth. He liked to whup me then rub some pepper on it. Seem like this Marster don't even talk mean."

"He does not believe in whipping," I said.

Cato grinned at this vision. "Now I hopes that is the gospel truth."

I do confess I think Cato will be a friend. *Bon nuit!*

Yours, &c.
Orrinda

September 1st, 1838

Crawford is ill. Perhaps with swamp fever. I would not know since I am not allowed to wait upon him. The Widow Turnwood frets I will catch the sickness, not being native to Louisiana. She assures me she nursed her husband all through his dying.

There is no greater hell than this. I cannot be satisfied mewed up here with my disordered heart. All night I stayed outside his door. I could feel Crawford waiting for me. Heard him saying: "Someone has hit me with a plank."

But *she* alone ministers to him and the house servants watch me. What can I do?

This afternoon I heard him retching, gasping for the strength to purge yet again, and I had to go to him. I could not keep no I couldn't from opening the door and finding the Widow wiping his mouth, bending to kiss his forehead.

"Orrinda." She reddened. "The draft!"

The draft indeed. That bedroom was as sealed as a tomb.

I wanted to put my hands about her neck and squeeze. Feel her Adam's apple under my thumbs. If he dies without me seeing him, I'll kill her.

My sole comfort is the now profuse Cato who at length declares: "It ain't Marster Fred's time."

Cato is the best of men. We did right to free him. I must protect Cato should Crawford die. But he can't. He has to live. Please God, let him live. Please, please, please. I'll do anything.

Cato's little boy was sold on the block a year ago. Their Master needed the money. The boy's name was Frank after Cato's baby brother who was whipped to death by their mistress. What kind of mother lashes another's baby dead? These sinners resound throughout Time. You put slivers of glass in their tea but they come again.

Strange to write twice in one day. I ought not. No. Tonight in the dark before morning again I heard singing. I opened my bedroom door to find Cato gone from his pallet in the hall. Not cool out now but the air has some ease and we sleep indoors. I went past the plantation hospital, the sufferers groaning with swelling, past the sugarhouse and stables. I could not be afraid following the hum for I was a perfect ghost myself, unable to see my hands before me.

A group of slaves stood in a ditch among pine-knot torches. Behind them, a slave graveyard full of wooden posts and crosses, names scratched with no dates. The preacher held up both palms, reading them as he swayed with his sermon, though his hands were naked of any book. When he finished he dropped to sitting on a log, his countenance bright with exultation. There was a shout: "The Debil has no place here!" The untiring congregation made a ring, shuffling right in a circle, the banjo talking and hands clapping. Daring to tap my foot ever so softly, I stood undetected in the brush, or so I imagined, when a field woman snatched up my arms, bending them back. "You ain't meant to be here," she said, glaring at me as if I had struck her.

"I'm looking for Cato," I insisted. "I'm not—"

"You ought not be here, Miss O." Cato came forward.

"Cato, I didn't mean to intrude," I said. "Only it is the most wonderful poetry!"

"Go on back to the house. I be up. Please, Miss O. You ain't supposed to be here."

Why stay when you are not wanted? Why did I bother to protest? Has it not always been my lot to be Apart?

Cato soon returned to the Great House, wavering in the bedroom doorway, contrite. "They ain't mean to go rough on you," he said.

I was sitting by the window. I kept my back to him, saying, "I had but little reason to expect otherwise."

"She didn't wanna hurt you none."

"There are few who don't," I said.

"Well I reckon I never knowed what folks is gonna do but I knows what you done for me. I told them how good you be—you an Marster Fred—how you done freed me."

I leapt up and shut the door. "Cato," I hissed, "no one is meant to know that! You could be in danger now."

"Miss O, I seed your heart and knowed you what they been praying for. Your reading in a few days?"

"Yes . . . why?" I asked.

"You seen what devilment that overseer up to. All my born days I met up with devils like he. They gon run, Miss O, but if we ain't help our brethren they can't ever get loose."

"Why? Isn't the Widow a kinder mistress than most?"

"But that damned overseer do as he please. He shot a nigger like she a horse. They mistress don't see what she don't care to. But all the white folks round here gon come hear you read."

"Don't remind me." I groaned, sitting back down by the window.

"They won't be recollecting their slaves, be busy listening to what joyment you gon preach. And since you a famous nigger, nobody but the house slaves set to watch you."

Our eyes met. "We can't. Not without—Cato listen, we have to wait to talk to Crawford. He'll help."

"They can't wait."

I looked away. "Well then they will be ravaged by dogs."

"You a mighty clever gal," he said.

"Is my vanity so transparent? Cato, I'm not that sort of clever. I'm a poet for Godsake. What on earth can I do?"

He stepped closer to me. "They needs guns," he said.

Outside, the slaves' singing stretched across the fields, catching and hanging in the trees.

"They'll be caught," I said.

Cato waited like he waits for Heaven.

"We might as well slit our necks tonight," I said.

Cato's face can have this embalmed despair.

"No women or children will be hurt?" I asked.

"I sees to it myself," Cato said.

Yours, &c.
Orrinda

Two new lines:

Hearing them hounds let loose in the night
Chasing the slave with the broken jaw

———

September 6th, 1836

A ghastly series of events. Where to begin? I suppose my tête-à-tête with the Widow Turnwood. She was greatly desirous of speaking with me before the reading. Again, I sat across from her in the parlor, the house women listening at the lock.

"Tonight at your reading there may be those very much opposed," she said.

"You must assure your neighbors it is only poetry," I said.

"I have tried to console myself with that very reasoning," she said, looking down at the fingers she had picked raw. The hem of her dress was filthy. "But you must realize that in these parts nobody lets their Negroes read or write, some even refuse to let them pray."

"Will they come then bearing clubs?" I smiled.

"Gracious, no! Not to this house. They have too much consideration for the memory of my husband. What I mean is that in their hearts, Orrinda, they are good people, and I have ever regarded that there are those among them, Christian souls, who deplore barbarity toward their slaves, and indeed, care for them as their own."

"Yet, I have heard that here a man was flogged for carrying a book which opposes slavery. I must tell you—I do not understand why you have asked me to come here."

She reached forward and picked up a copy of my book from the table. "When my husband died last year, I was wholly alone. A cousin of mine in New York sent me books, yours among them. Your words seemed to understand just how alone. Imagine my disbelief to find that you were a slave! And when I wrote to Mr. Crawford, he was convinced that we must meet. I can tell you that you have my word as a Christian that I will safeguard you tonight. And if something were to befall Mr. Crawford, I will see you and Cato safely to Boston. For it wouldn't be safe for two slaves to travel there alone."

"Yes," I said, staring at the wall.

There it was again.

"You are too kind," I said.

That word again.

"I must go," I stood.

O I had heard it the first time she had said it, but now there was no mistaking that the Widow Turnwood believed me a Slave.

I found Crawford convalescing in the library, his feet up, and the sun a bright square on his chin. I shut the door, my stomach in my chest.

He turned his head, and there is no more overworked, apt word for it—he looked quite beautiful there in the light.

"You seem severe," he said. "What have I done now?"

"Are we free?" I asked. "And I beg you will tell me the truth."

"What's the matter?" He set his feet down. "Are you crying?"

"Is Cato truly free? Did you free him?"

"Of course," Crawford said. "I thought we agreed not to publicize it until safely above the Mason-Dixon. For Godsake, Orrinda, if you are going to have some sort of hysterical outbur—"

"Am I?" I pressed my hand to my heart and could feel the beat in my head.

"Is this a fit of nerves?" he smiled.

"Crawford," I said. "Crawford."

His face was all eyes. "Why on earth are you asking me that?"

"I'm not." I covered my face. "Oh God, I'm not . . ."

I turned into a blunt gas meant to wander for all eternity in a sick fog.

Crawford was up on his feet, bustling me away from the door, whispering fiercely: "Listen, I will explain it. Listen, in Boston, what did it matter? Being a free state: you *were* free. It was my intention to get the papers, I swear to you, but out of sheer neglect, sloth really! I didn't. A sin for which I pray you'll forgive, and you will, Orrinda, you must. For it was not to own you, never to own you. I didn't even remember that you were anything but free until Anthea, I mean, Mrs. Turnwood invited us South. My deceit, my only deceit—for to utterly protect you as you are not kin to me—was to leave you a slave so that no one here can lawfully harm you. I realize the false wisdom of this but—"

"Crawford," I said, "you are telling me that you haven't found the chance to file my papers in sixteen years? How can I believe you even if I wanted to?" I turned from him and back toward the door.

He stepped in front of me. "Orrinda, you needn't be jealous."

"O but who could come between us?" I pushed past. "We are joined by the letter of the law."

"We can leave," he said to my back.

I stopped.

He came to me and took my hands. "Listen." He squeezed. "Listen."

"Let go," I said, but my arms were too weak to pull away.

"We will leave right this moment," he said.

I stared at him. "Are you mad? The reading is in a matter of hours."

"Whatever you want, I shall do it. I swear."

I tried to read his face. "But you lie so easily," I said. "You are a liar. You would leave without the money? You?"

"I will do as you wish. I swear upon my life."

Of course, I wanted to run. Run until we can't, until we fall into the sea and are extinguished by unforgiving waves. But I thought then of the slaves laboring in the fields, blood flowing as freely as heat, and how only I could give them guns.

I pulled my hands out of his. "I'll do the reading. We'll get our money. Then we leave."

"Good girl." He smiled, drying my cheek with a handkerchief that smelled faintly of eggs.

I hate him. He purports to be my liberator, my ever-abiding champion, but it has never been true. A slave can be beaten, branded, flogged, shot, raped, maimed for the slightest infraction imagined or real. A slave is starved of all sustenance, body and soul, which would allow them to feel free to be human. I have never not been this thing—slave—that corrupts all things. How is it that I love the man who keeps me a thing, which can be beaten, branded, flogged, shot, raped, maimed, burned, gouged, flayed, killed . . . ?

He picked up the novel he had been reading off the floor. "*Charlotte Temple* again. Dreadfully overblown." He tried to laugh.

"I want to go to my room."

He stepped aside and I went toward the door. "Wait," he said. "You will forgive me, eventually, won't you?"

I kept walking.

"You should know my will says you are to be emancipated at my death."

"O?" I whispered without turning, "Is that what it is to be adored?"

I felt I was walking over glass to get out of the house and into the sun where somewhere in the sugar a slave was screaming. O for a life where I were invisible! Where I were the color of air! But I am the nethermost of all the earth's creatures: a Brown Woman. And how the world wishes to punish me for being born to these two sins!

When the housekeeper secreted me a set of keys, I marched into the Widow Turnwood's bedroom and searched it from top to bottom. For tomorrow's moonless night, I gave the slaves three guns.

I don't care what they do with them. I don't care if they shoot us all. Such is the daily horror of their existence, which so we passively witness, that they should make our world a hell and then we will know what God is.

Yours, &c.
Orrinda

———

September 7th, 1836

I have come to my Bad End.

Tonight thirty-odd neighbors gathered. Expectation riot in the parlor. A room holding villains and well-wishers both. I stood at the podium where too many men eased near, their eyes telling me of a cold desire to mutilate my flesh. The Widow Turnwood hovered in the corner by the tea, aghast at her own misbegotten temerity. But all the flaxen hair in the world could not hide her.

Crawford, the showman who figured himself the

conduit, the vampire who flattered himself a prophet, delivered an introduction evoking me as a stunted Athena, an obedient goddess, never surpassing the miniature form born of his thigh.

We had agreed that I would perform only Nature poems: those limited, early works of lyrical mimickings and indulgent odes to America's landscapes. Verse which asks no questions, has no economy, and is but a blundered attempt at metaphysical complexity—the dregs of my youth.

After my first poem, not a soul clapped but the Widow: my graceless, beleaguered benefactress whose mind is not half as sharp as her heart. In the ensuing silence after my second poem (the Widow having exhausted her defiance), I paused, spying a black man at the back of the audience. This man was not known to me. I wondered why had he not gone with the other slaves and prayed Cato far afield.

Yet this did not occasion my revolt. For indeed, even in that horrified delay did I intend to be good. Did I not open with "I Walked in Cambridge" followed by "Thou Art My Ode"? I would have been a perfect paragon of black redemption had I not seen a slave child darting down the corridor of oak trees after his elders through the window behind the rows of simmering white faces. I knew then why I am here. Knew I must speak, though it bring the walls down about me. Knew I have been afraid to be seen fully, to have my heart exposed with all its merciless sorrow for unnamed blood spilling even now, easily and unjustly, into the ground.

"I hope," I said without looking at the crowd, "you

will humbly permit me to share my newest work. It is
an early sketch. I beg you will pardon its rough edges."

Then I looked at the one I thought I loved most in
this world, my master, Mr. Frederick Crawford, whose
gray eyes communicated a horror transparent.

> *Lord, You alone have chosen me, yet*
> *This ornate darkness keeps me from sleep*
> *Hearing them hounds let loose in the night*
> *Chasing the slave with the broken jaw*
> *Who was salted in the sun.*
> *You will know him by his sin*
> *Tell the Lord, he is coming,*
> *Tell his son he is dead and gone*
> *Throw his boy three times over him*
> *Gather stones to hold down his grave*
> *Because it has begun to rain*

I did not see the man who sent his fist. I tasted only
the blood he left. I buckled under the bitter heat in my
mouth. I screamed for Crawford, but people swelled
the room. Down behind the podium, a man caught me
about the neck. He was older than I had imagined my
murderer to be. With deaf blue eyes and a grandfather's
belly, his knees went between my legs as he punched me
in the head. But there was a gunshot and my would-be
murderer released me. As I raised myself to my elbows
I saw the slave who had been at the back of the audience
holding a gun. He shot the overseer then fired wildly
into the crowd. A neighbor shot him in the chest,
but the slave only fell to his knees and with a jubilant

scream found and shot his mistress. The Widow Turnwood fell like a child slipping down the stairs. Crawford ran to her and the neighbor shot him in the head. Crawford landed on his back, his leg bent under him, bleeding onto the already crimson carpet.

How long I was alone in time. How long held there. Alone.

There was a corpse near my shoulder. I knew I had to wipe my hands in its blood, to paint myself dead and lay facedown so that when men came across me, I was fortunate that they kicked me until they believed me only a body. Realizing that there was not a living slave left to kill, they ushered out their women and furiously mounted their horses to fetch their hounds for the hunt.

When finally the Great House went quiet, I crawled out. "Crawford?" I called for no reason at all for I could see him lying in a circle drawn by overturned chairs and the trampled pages of my poetry. He was a heap, made innocent by the hole in the back of his head. His nose and eyes bleeding profusely. I tried to keep in the blood. I tried. But you have to be a god.

"You ought not move him, Miss O," Cato said, kneeling next to me.

I grabbed him by both shoulders. "What are you doing here? They'll come back!"

"I ain't sees George," he said, looking down at Crawford. "I knew he had a gun so I come back to fetch him. And now Marster Fred bout to go on to his just reward."

For a moment I could not get my voice out. "Who is George?" I said.

Cato pointed to the dead slave. "Ise reckon can't blame the man."

"Listen."

He shook his head. "That overseer kilt his wife giving her bout five hundred lashes. Cut to bone."

"Cato. Listen. You've been very brave. But that's over now. Get me paper I'll write you a pass. Perhaps you could make it to Boston, to Crawford's family. They'll help you. They're abolitionists. I'll write them a letter. There must be paper in the desk."

"Laws." He shooed me.

"Please do as I say! I don't want to see what they'll do to you. George is dead, Crawford's practically dead, the Widow's dead—we're all dead, but not you, not yet."

"Can't run without you, Miss O."

I pushed at him. "Go on! You're free!"

"We both free," he said.

I choked out a laugh. "No, not me. I'm a slave till he's dead. Crawford never freed me. And the irony is that still I cannot leave him here to die alone."

Cato looked down at his hands. "Ise awful sorry."

"I'll be fine. Just go."

Cato nodded slowly. "You right. But could I look at your writings for I go? Always did want to see your words."

"But you can't read," I said, looking down at Crawford who was not quite dead but so close to dying I could not believe it. "O, what does it matter," I said to him and Cato. "We must hurry."

I found my journal on the floor by the podium. As I picked it up, I turned to see Cato take out one of the guns I'd given him and shoot Crawford twice in the chest.

I have always thought, well someday he will die, Crawford will die, no matter how I love him he will. But I had hoped it would at least be far away when I would not know it, and here he went and exited without one word to me of how I should live.

I screamed and dogs howled and Cato rushed me out to where the fields were sweetly burning.

In the smoke I cried, "Will we get free?"

"If not in this world then for sho the next," Cato said.

And now we run for our lives.

Yours, &c.
Orrinda

James III

I hustled left at the car dealership, picking my way over the loose gravel in the road, hopping up on the concrete bridge to the safety of the smooth. I stopped running when I got to the top of the station steps and took advantage of my inhalerless wheezing and checked out the platform situation. No one but a dude in a black baseball cap, tattoos up his neck. He was circling the telephone pole, eating (I am nearsighted) fries?

"Damn," the boy swallowed at me as I stepped down onto the wooden train platform. I was barefoot in November and way too fat to hide.

"I'm good," I said. I even managed to shrug.

He stared at the blood and boogers weighing down my upper lip. I wiped at it with my sweatshirt sleeve, which was still too big for me and hung over my hands, meaning I hadn't grown this fall, meaning puberty was still avoiding me like I was some amateur stalker. "Yo, can I git some of those napkins?" I asked without crying.

He furnished me with a hamburger'd stack. "Man"—he popped in a definite fry—"you got your ass beat. Oh shit, they take yo shoes too? Damn, that's some Oliver Twist shit right there. Know what you need?" He finished off the last of his soda.

"Mr. Brownlow," I said, referring to the old man who saves Oliver in Dickens.

"Who?" he asked.

"No one," I said.

"You need ice." He offered me his cup. "You shaking, man."

"I'm shivering," I corrected him and sat down on the bench so I could steady my elbows on my knees. Now that I'd stopped running I was cold, the hair at the back of my neck damp and spiraling tight.

"Damn." He sat down next to me. "You just a little dude. Your feet don't even touch the ground."

There was no point dignifying that with a response so I merely emptied the ice out onto two napkins. It was a common/alienating observation better ignored. If I wasn't being called gay or a little bitch while getting punched in the side of the head like I used to at my old school, my policy was to let that shit slide.

"This the wrong time of year to get your shoes took. And I'm thinking your nose might could be broke. It's all cut right there." He demonstrated on his.

"I know." I casually turned away from him, sliding the ice to that spot.

"What grade you in?"

"Ninth."

"Ninth? You don't look like you in ninth. You go to Lower Merion? You know a dude named Tyrese?"

"No." I was so cold I couldn't feel my toes.

"Where you go?"

"Friends." I reached down and squeezed them, even though I could barely feel my fingers either.

"What? I said where you go."

"Friends. It's a Quaker school. Kinda religious, namsayin."

"Like the oats? Like—what's that old dude's name? Benjamin Franklin!" He leaned back. "Bennie, the man on the big bill." He wiped his hands on his jeans then turned his baseball cap around.

"He wasn't a Quaker," I said.

"What y'all's beliefs?"

"I don't know. I just go there." I really did not feel like talking about peace and justice right that minute.

"You don't know?" he repeated, my fictitious ignorance paining him.

"I'm not a Quaker," I snapped, looking down the tracks for the train.

"How long you been going there?"

"Since sixth grade," I muttered.

"Sixth grade? Then you best know!"

I sighed. "Man . . ." and switched up napkins. "In the priesthood of all believers. The light of God in everyone. Service. Peace." My stomach did a hari-kari. I had to go to the bathroom real bad.

He thought/chewed the lone, brown shrimp'd french fry left in his bag. "Yeah. That's deep, man. I'm interested in shit like that. Quakers. I'm Wallace."

"James."

"Train's coming." Wallace hopped up and shot his bag into the trash can as the light of the train pushed through the dark to find us. "You going home?"

I thought of how upstairs my little brother had been crying like he knew I was the only one who could hear him. "No." I slipped off the bench, scanning the gloomily fluorescent parking lot. None of the cars were Mom's. I knew she wouldn't come but I had thought somehow she might come. "I can't," I told the light posts, the empty cars, the white paint keeping them apart.

"Ey!" Wallace waved at me from the yellow-painted edge of the platform.

I limped across the freezing concrete. "You think the conductor will be okay with letting me on?"

"You ain't contagious, is you?"

"I'm serious, man."

Wallace looked me up and down. "You best throw them nasty-ass napkins in the trash. And roll up yo sleeves—you don't want to be looking like you killed nobody."

"I meant I'm not wearing shoes," I said as I hopped from foot to foot, trying to fight frostbite.

"So?" He was mystified.

"Ain't that illegal?"

"What you mean?"

"Not wearing shoes in a public place—ain't that illegal?"

He lifted his eyebrows. "You weird."

Well, shit was weird. I had no phone, no shoes, no glasses. Nothing but a ten-dollar bill in my khakis. But even though I might've looked like a crackhead, I was more like a martyr, and ten dollars were enough to get me to Aunt Bernice.

As the train cars rattled by, Wallace said, "Here man, let me give you my card." He handed me a glossy black business card. "You might be in need of my services."

The train stopped and the conductor stepped out as I turned

the card over. "This just has your name and e-mail. What services do you offer?"

"Son, you name it, I can provide. For a price," he said and hopped up on the steps.

On the train, Wallace swung into his own seat, stretching his legs across the cracking blue vinyl. I took the row behind him and put up my hood worrying, would Mrs. P. give me another extension on my courtly love paper? She liked me. Thought I was the next Terrance Hayes. I didn't know who that was but I told her Yeah. Ostensibly, I would have to lean on this scholastic partiality.

Wallace pushed himself up so his chin hooked the top of the seat. "Man, let me tell you one thing."

I was stroking my nose, trying to find which part hurt the worst. As my skin began to thaw, my ears burned.

"Pain lets you know you alive," he said and flopped back down.

I exchanged glances with my reflection and wished I could talk to my dad.

Sometimes at night I woke with my back stuck to the sheet, remembering finding Dad asleep on the couch. I guess him and Mom were having issues even then. The windows open and a white curtain blowing on his face. Air so cold it was wet.

"Dad?"

In Grandmomma's stories, men died of drafts. Sometimes they'd crossed an Obeah woman, or been cursed by some dude in love with their wife. But most times the draft meant a duppy was coming cuz somewhere, sometime these men had done something bad.

I slammed the window shut to wake him.

"J?" Dad said, hitting back the curtain. "What you doing?"

"Why are you sleeping on the couch?"

"Your mother said I was snoring."

I saw he was still wearing his shoes. "Where were you?"

"Out. Why you up?"

I'd knelt at his head, knowing he might dodge/comfort me. "I'm thinking bad thoughts."

"Again? Boy, you know you got to get your sleep. You got school in the morning." He made room for me on the couch.

"What do I do?" I asked, getting under.

"Think good thoughts." He'd yawned, tucking me in.

Sometimes at night, I imagined he was still there sleeping under the white curtain in that cold, safe room.

When we got to Suburban Station, I saw Mom in the crowd on the platform. A copper-headed woman getting on as I was about to step off. I pushed my way to her, knowing it was impossible, but because I have never not known her, I sometimes made her have superhero powers. When I squeezed close enough to brush her coat, I didn't need my glasses to see that this lady couldn't have even been Mom's cousin. She wasn't black—she was like Mexican or something.

"Ey, James!" Wallace called down to me from the escalator as it carried him up and into the city. He grinned as my eyes found him. "You alive, son! You alive!"

According to the homies in puffy coats on the plastic chairs around their stoop who took one look at my nose and agreed

I was too fucked up to fuck with, it was eight-thirty at night. On the real though, I had found and tied two plastic bags over my feet, was legally blind, and all I had left in the world were bloodstained sweatpants with seven dollars and fifty cents in them. And still, I didn't cry. I did have this feeling like I was being followed, but when I randomly/anxiously turned, all I saw was that the way I had come was dark.

I hobbled down Fitzwater and Eighteenth, passing flat-fronted brick row houses with long white windows and worn stone steps on my way to Aunt B's. But my rush was in vain: no one was home. Not even a damn Welcome mat for my ass. I slumped on the bottom step, perching my Pathmark heels on some weeds coming up out of the sidewalk and wiped at my dripping/clogged nose. There was no way I was gonna cry even though I was kind of starting to cry.

Self-snitching: crying had been a problem since I was nine. But back then, people were cool with it. I had earned my tears. Cuz when I was nine, my dad went to prison, my parents got divorced, and Mom and me moved out of Philly to her ex-boyfriend's house in Bryn Mawr. But three years later to still be getting all inconsolable about negligible shit? Like when I misspelled *remainder* on the floor of the State Spelling Bee? (A gaffe I ascribe to it being 6 A.M. and a fear of large white crowds.) I mean, people at Friends paid more in tuition than people in my old school paid for rent in a year—what was to cry over now?

The fuzz of a woman in lavender scrubs with some animal on them stood over me. "Lord child, you scared me." Aunt Bernice hugged me quick but just as quick pulled back. "What happened to your face?"

The concern in my aunt's voice disturbed my weak hold on ocular dignity. "Nothing." I looked down. "I got in a fight after school. Tenth graders. Way bigger than me."

Aunt Bernice turned my chin as my cousin, Nahala, slammed the car door, saying, "Oo you got hit good, huhn?"

"Your nasal passages blocked?" asked my aunt, decorously ignoring my cousin.

"Not really," I said.

Then in rapid fire: "You been throwing up? Your neck hurt? This happened at your school? Does your mother know?"

I thought back to Mom, waiting in the pickup line at school, the flags at the top of the flagpole on the side of the gym snapping. I had spotted her leaning out the window of our black SUV in aviator sunglasses, seeing me and smiling then spitting out her gum. Behind her was Jacquon, trapped in his car seat, looking happy to see me when I climbed in front and gummy smiling to let out some drool. Today it had seemed like going home would be okay. I wondered what Jacquon was doing.

"She ain't home yet," I said. "She went out. To dinner. With a friend."

Aunt Bernice unlocked the door. "Well, it don't look too crooked."

Soon I was deep in the scratchy cushions of Aunt Bernice's couch where back in the day I had made some dope-ass forts. I swaddled myself in one of Grandmomma's quilts with an ice pack until Nahala tickled my feet.

"Stop it." I kicked.

"You were dreaming," she said.

"I'm just resting my eyes."

"Ew, you sweating over everything."

"No, I'm not." I sat up and my damp sweatshirt peeled from my back.

"You can't call or nothing before you come over? This ain't no motel."

"I forgot my phone," I said.

Aunt Bernice came out from the kitchen where she was reheating coffee. "Nahala, give your cousin a clean shirt and socks."

"You forgot your shoes too?"

I looked at my dirty cracked feet. "They stole them."

"Sure," drawled Nahala. "C'mon. Somebody have to kill me before I let them take my shoes." I followed her into her room where she had flung open her closet. "First, we need to get you up out of that crusty-ass sweatshirt."

I sat on her bed and raised the hoodie she'd thrown at me to my eyes. Just as I'd suspected: glitter. "This is not really me," I said.

"You right, beige isn't so good with your skin. You darker than your mom. Yasmine kinda look mixed."

"So?" I heard a dish fall without breaking in the kitchen.

"So what you need"—she said *need* too loud—"is bright colors."

Aunt Bernice stepped in holding a thermos. "J, you want to come and have them take a look at your nose? Nahala, don't you have something a little more . . . for a man in there."

"Not that are gonna fit his fat ass," my cousin said.

"Girl, ain't nothing ever easy with you. Just find him something in my stuff. It'd be good to have a doctor make sure, honey," she said to me.

"It doesn't hurt anymore," I said.

"I find that hard to believe. I've got to get to work. Call your mother and let her know what's going on," Aunt Bernice said and went out.

Nahala listened for the front door then rolled her head to me. "I know, you know."

"What are you talking about?"

"I know what goes down in yo house. Yasmine told me Karl's been tripping. But she let him beat on you?"

"I don't know what you mean."

"I mean, you ain't his son. But none of this would've happened if she hadn't got up in his face."

"Who?"

"Your moms." She made a sound of disgust. "Nigga, don't play dumb. If you wanna be with a crazy-ass dude like Karl, you don't go popping off at the mouth."

"You're retarded," I said, my face blank/combusting.

"I'm not the issue. I'm the type of chick dealing with what God's given me. Your mom—"

"Shut up!" I rolled up and ran blindly at Nahala, trying to ram her backward into the closet, but she reached up and grabbed the top of the door frame and thrust me back with her foot so that I fell and rolled off the bed.

"Oh hell no! Ain't you had your ass beat enough already? Come on now, I ain't about to fight no nine-year-old."

"I'm twelve," I fumed, scrambling up.

She patted the bed. "Come on, I ain't mad at ya. Look J, all I was trying to say was that I feel yo mom. I do. Yasmine just trying to hold down her man. I mean, she has love for you, obviously. But who you think is paying for your fancy-ass school?"

"I have a scholarship." I stayed where I was.

"That don't pay for it all."

"My dad pays the rest."

Nahala snorted. "Yo dad can't pay for a phone call. My mom puts money in his account every month. Your dad . . . listen to your cheesy ass." She slapped her thigh, cackling.

I digested this. Then my next step was clear. "I'll pay you to take me to see my dad."

"Boy you must be out your mind."

"Fifty dollars. C'mon, you're eighteen, you can take me. Please?"

"You got fifty dollars?"

"Not on me—at home."

"Who you foolin?" she said.

"Seventy-five? I swear I have it. Drive me in the morning when your mom's asleep."

"Seventy-five dollars?" She pretended to hesitate. "Karl do this to you?"

"Maybe." I sat down on the corner of her bed, pressing my nose where it hurt the most. "Maybe I did something to him."

"Yeah, right," she said and pulled a suitcase down from the shelf at the top of her closet. "I got something that'll fit you." She unzipped it and threw me a shirt. I put it to my face. The letters N.W.A.

"This is yours?" I asked, surprised.

"Your dad's."

"It's dope." I swallowed and was glad to be blind, running down the hall and into the bathroom where I squeezed his T-shirt to my chest and did not cry.

⚏

We drove our dead granddaddy's faded blue Buick sedan over an hour and a half to get to the prison in a rain that cut silver.

We didn't try to talk over the acrobatics of the radio's R&B until the storm got so heavy Nahala had to pull over. She turned the radio off and we passed a two-liter bottle of Cherry Coke back and forth, listening to the beating the roof was taking.

"This kind of weather gets me moody." Nahala burped and began picking at the steering wheel. "Thunder in the morning. Don't make no sense."

"Stop hogging." I pulled the bottle from her. "How old is this car?"

"Older than both us put together."

"What if the roof starts leaking?"

"Hope you can swim." She handed me the bottle cap. "Why didn't you call your mom?"

"Why didn't she call me?"

"You think she knows you with us?"

"Why not." I put my forehead to the window, looking up into a sky of dirty-looking rain. Sometimes after one of her fights with Karl, Mom would come up into my bedroom and look at me like she didn't know which one of us was in trouble. "She's probably fine," I said.

"Damn, now I got to pee. You seen bruises?" Nahala asked.

"Not on her face." A red smear of brake lights glowed in front of us.

"What about Jacquon?"

"Never." I flushed and right away I could picture his sad face—how he pushed his bottom lip out before he cried. "Karl's never touched Jacquon."

"Not yet."

"I couldn't take him—he's a baby and I'm a kid. Mom will watch out for him."

Nahala gave me a look. I pointed to the car in front of us. "I believe they're moving," I said and turned up the music until I couldn't hear the rain.

"Hi," I said to my dad/mystery man who was a hunched blur behind the Plexiglas. "What's up?" Meaning I had totally forgotten what to say. Maybe this was the wrong move. What could Dad do? He was more helpless than me: a neon'd prisoner of the state, segregated from my low-grade worries.

Nahala snatched the phone from me. "Hi Uncle James." She handed it back, still facing my dad but eavesdropping on the girl next to us crooning to her man.

"I want to know what's up with you," he said to me.

"I don't know. I just wanted to see you, I guess."

"Now you see me."

"No, I don't actually," I said.

"What happened?"

"I don't have my glasses."

"Son. What happened to your face?"

"I got in a fight."

"At school?" He sounded surprised. "Ain't they supposed to be teaching you to turn the other cheek?"

"This kid, this big kid, he—"

"Nigga"—Nahala smacked my shoulder—"I ain't drove your ass down here for you to lie."

The phone line went silent/aggrieved.

"You know why you named James?" he asked.

"No," I sulked into my T-shirt, then mumbled, "after you."

"And I'm named after my father, your granddaddy. Now that man? That man was born evil and done stayed that way. But because he was named James, I got named James, and your grandmomma said you got to be named James that way at the end of the day you got his hard and my heart. You James the third."

"Dad, to be honest—"

"Finally," said Nahala.

"I came here to tell you I need to move back to Philly. Can I move in with Aunt Bernice? Say yes."

"What's wrong with living with your mother?" he asked.

"I hate that bitch."

"Yo! Who you talking to with that mouth? That's not being how I taught you to be."

Even Nahala looked at me with big NO eyes.

"You know what that fight did to you?" he said. "It put fear back in your heart. Last thing you need is move back to Philly. Now what's your name?"

"Dad." I thumped my fist on the counter.

"Boy, I want to hear that name out yo mouth."

"James Marcus King the third."

"Amen," said Nahala.

"At least those rich kids ain't packing nine millimeters," he said.

I folded my arms over my chest. "All I want is to live in Philly with Aunt Bernice, is that so much to ask?"

"Why? Why do you want that so bad?"

I said nothing, listening to the beat of my heart. Even though it was November, the AC was blowing morgue breath down my neck, and this time I knew who the duppy was hunting.

"Now I realize you probably think because I'm in here I can't help you, right?"

"It's not that. It's . . ." I wished I could see his eyes properly.

"What? Ain't nothing you can't tell me."

"Okay." I took a breath. "At school, they tell us violence is a short-term satisfaction, and I know that's right, the right thing, but what about defending someone you love? I mean, you're not supposed to do anything? You're just supposed to stand by and watch them get killed?"

"Who's getting killed?"

"It's hypothetical, Dad."

"Your mother? What you really talking about is revenge, son. You want to hurt them for the hurt they just did, but even if you f—muff them up, that don't heal the first hurt. That's done. That's past. Now you just like them: somebody who hurts people."

I felt like he wasn't really getting me. "But if someone was hurting me wouldn't you—"

"What? Wouldn't I what?" he asked all wild.

"If someone was trying to kill me, Dad . . . wouldn't you?" But I couldn't say it. How could I—being there—say it?

He was holding the phone with both hands. "If something was ever to go down, to happen to my son? Man, I just couldn't be in this world . . ." he trailed/choked.

"Dad?" I gripped the phone tight.

"I just hate seeing you like this, man. Bad enough I can't hug you or even shake yo hand, but now I got to see you all busted up and I can't do nothing? You know I live for my kid." He covered his face.

"Uncle James?" asked Nahala.

"Dad?" His head was down. "It's just my nose! I mean, I'm alive, I'm okay. Right? Dad?"

"Oh you gon be okay." He looked up, wiping his face. "We is making sho of that. Now you tell me exactly what happened."

"James," said Nahala. "James," said my dad.

But when I opened my mouth there was a God-robbing crack in my chest and I knew that my life was not ever gonna come correct. So I put my head down on the counter so no prison dudes would see and cried like a nine-year-old into the phone to my dad.

Yesterday I was at home with my dresser against the door, Petrarch on my lap, and Mom downstairs in Where Were You Bitch? (featuring Karl). I was listening, trying to figure out if the crashing was bodies or furniture, and at the same time read the *Rime Sparse*.

I went into the hall. Why? Cuz my little half brother was crying and I didn't want Karl to come up. Even though it was November in Bala Cynwyd, I was sweating in the house's sunless heat debating whether or not to call the police. In his room, Jacquon was in his crib, snuffling on his fuzzy red back, gumming the corner of a soft plastic book.

I went in his room. "What's good, little man?"

He stopped chewing and rolled toward me, blinking at me through the wooden bars.

"Hi," I whispered and picked him up, his big ol head still wobbly so I cradled him in my arms.

A door slammed and Mom, high on Prosecco, was shouting.

"How's life in the crib?" I set him back down to pick his pacifier up off the rug and rubbed the carpet fuzz off with my sleeve, wishing Mom and Karl would die/vanish and then Jacquon and me could live with Aunt Bernice until I was eighteen and we moved into my place. Downstairs, furniture began to slide and Jacquon's gold eyes went all portentous. "You okay," I said and rubbed his little back and wound his mobile of fluffy baby birds so they sang and spun, but then Mom screamed and we screamed too.

Then I was standing in the middle of their bedroom holding the phone. But it felt like a toy cause Mom's crying was louder than any dial tone. Soon my hands were pushing through Karl's magazines until they found his gun, black and shining at the bottom of his nightstand drawer. As I skidded down the hall, I passed by Jacquon, sitting up in his crib and as our eyes met, I glanced/transmitted: Look, I'm sorry I'm about to shoot your dad but I'm doing it before he kills our mom. A lot of that might of got lost in translation (him being before language as he was), but I swear we had an agreement.

At the top of the stairs, I was still in the place of where I might not do it. But as I walked down, the gun behind my back, I saw Karl's big square head over my mom as he choked her on our hand-knotted New Zealand wool door mat. All I could do was point the gun and close my eyes, wishing as I pulled that we all died and reappeared somewhere easy.

There was a metal roar and I opened my eyes. Karl was standing up, his mouth dropped, looking at a bullet buried in the wall to his right. "What the fuck?" he shouted.

Both of them were looking at me, alive and angry.

"James?" Mom coughed, crawling against the foyer wall. I tripped down the stairs, gun out, coming at Karl until it poked his chest.

"Calm down, man." Karl tried to back away.

"James!" Mom was up and her hand was out. "You give me that gun!"

But I lifted it to Karl's head. I just wanted him to go away forever. I didn't care how—just away.

"Listen to your mother, man," he said. "You're a—a good kid."

"James!" My mom tried to get my attention. "I don't want anybody getting hurt."

I looked over at the charms which had pierced so many: the Curtises, the Rashans, the Calvins, the Rays and Derays. But that hair coppered, those breasts immoveable, thus a body to make any video vixen anxious, meant nothing to me. "She is your mother," Dad had said when they were taking him off to prison. "She is your diamond. You take care of her for me. You're the James of the house now—" and he had smiled to show me that he believed I could do it. I looked at my mother, saw the left side of her mouth cut red and her cheek swelling elastic, and I told her, "But Mom, you're hurt."

As I was looking at her, Karl punched me in the face. My glasses bit under my eye and my nose cracked. Without thinking, I hit him with the gun as he was coming at me, smashing whatever I could until he went away, then I dropped back, cupping my screaming nose.

When I wiped my stinging eyes, I could make out Mom bending over him, seeing if *he* was okay, begging, "Karl? Karl?"

He shoved her off, cradling his head as he sank to his knees.

"Mom?" I called to her from where I was on the floor.

She stumbled over and lifted my chin, her gold necklace penduluming into the blue silk of her shirt. "Oh baby—" She hesitated to touch the swelling between my eyes. "Your nose."

I took her hand. "Let's get Jacquon and go."

She snatched it back. "We got to get you some ice." She tried to wipe the blood from my nose with the bottom of her shirt.

"Ow! Stop!"

She cringed. "Does it hurt?"

"No it feels amazing!"

"Boy, this is no time for attitude," she snapped, then stood wringing her hands. "Shit, shit! What am I gonna do?"

"Let's go!"

"I can't." She covered her face then straightened. "I'll get you some ice. Stay here."

"Can't you at least call the police?" I yelled at her as she rushed toward the kitchen.

Karl tried to get up without falling. There was a trickle of blood coming from a dent on his forehead.

"Mom?" I was on my feet. The room tilted and I remembered the gun. "Mom?" I called again, frantically looking around the foyer. Nothing on the hardwood but the rug and my broken glasses.

"What?" Mom hurried back in. "What's wrong?" She eyed Karl and grabbed my arm. "Come in the kitchen with me, c'mon!"

"You're dead, man," moaned Karl.

Mom changed direction, pulling me with her. "This way."

"Stop," I hissed as she tried to wrestle me to the front door. She angled it open. I dug my fingers into the doorframe. "The gun!"

"I have it—" She pushed me out the door and I spilled onto the front step, my hands slapping the chilled concrete, the door slamming behind me. I lay there in my blood/defeat, listening to dogs bark somewhere in our cul-de-sac.

And when Jacquon's cries appeared, they were little paper airplanes over my head, and like the ones at school, somehow they always find me. I forgot about Mom—she was an adult, she could take care of herself—all I wanted was to go back in for my little brother so I got up and beat on the door until I heard Karl scream, "That's him! Motherfucker, I'm gonna kill you!"

My legs went seasick, blood stopped going to my brain, and my stomach started signaling a loss of control in my bowels, cuz the duppy was there behind that door, ready to drag me toward death where I would forget my name.

What happened, Dad? I left. Because the body betrays, forgets us—who we are, who we love—saves itself and what we think the world is melts like crayons that leave no mark but a mess. I didn't faint; didn't pee my pants; I ran. My legs pumped and the blood rushed up from my stomach to my head.

Of course I thought of them as I ran, thought of calling the cops, of going back, but instead I told myself that they'd be okay cuz at the end of the day Mom said she had the gun.

∎⟁

We left the prison and hours later I was cutting across our yard in Nahala's too-small flip-flops, lifting the pouting stone cherub on the porch for the spare key. A neighbor two houses down was backing out of his driveway and seeing me, braked. I stood there, staring through the gnats playing over the flat-top hedges, waiting for his window but he just rolled out with a screech down the cul-de-sac. I went to the doorstep where Wallace and Nahala stood in the rude chatter of birds. An SUV was in the driveway.

"This is a bad idea," said Nahala, done pounding on the door. "I don't think she's home. Imma call your mom again."

"I got the key. It's all good," I said.

"Oh yeah?" she asked. "Then why we got him here?"

Wallace looked down at her from his almost impressive height. "For protection," he said.

"How much you getting?" she asked.

"Fifty."

"Fifty?" She laughed.

"Nahala! That's all I have," I told Wallace. "I'm broke y'all, broke."

"J, let's just go. Wait till your dad speaks with your mom."

"When's that gonna happen? He can't call her, she has to call him. She won't do it."

"Look, you can stay at my house forever—I don't care."

"He want to make sure his mom's okay. Girl," Wallace said, "you ain't got to worry when I'm around."

"Whatever." Nahala rolled her eyes.

I put the key in the lock. Maybe I was thinking if I could just get into bed and go to sleep, I would wake up and nothing bad would have happened. But when I got upstairs Jacquon's crib was empty, his little striped dog lying on its side. My room was how I'd left it: Petrarch's sonnets facedown on the bed. Downstairs, I heard Nahala calling Hello?

"This some Quaker shit?" Wallace appeared behind me and picked up the book.

"No. I was supposed to be writing a paper about courtly love. But it was due today so . . ."

"Too late," he said.

Nahala came running up the stairs. "No one. Let's go. It's freezing in here. Jacquon at day care?"

I wondered if I'd ever see my little brother again. "Probably," I said, coasting down the hall like I was sitting in a hovering armchair. I wandered toward the cracked door of Mom and Karl's bedroom.

"Go on," said Nahala, "Open it."

My stomach somersaulted and landed wrong on its back. "You do it," I told Wallace.

"It's your house," he said.

"Ain't I paying you?"

"Y'all chicken." Nahala put a hand on the door, then paused. "J, maybe you should close your eyes."

"Why?" asked Wallace, uncomfortable.

"Yeah why, Nahala? I can't even see."

"Cuz you just a kid."

We all stared at her hand, shrinking back from the door as it opened like tourists at a zoo with no cages. But there was nothing inside except bedsheets feeding a pile of clothes on the floor.

"See! Nothing," said Nahala.

"I'm gonna see if my glasses are downstairs," I announced, heading down the hall.

Wallace followed. "Ain't they smashed?"

"Maybe I can tape them."

Nahala grabbed my elbow. "I'm ready to leave."

"Why?" I asked/taunted, letting Wallace step in front of me.

"Because it feels like a haunted house up in here." She took my hand going down the stairs. "I don't even like scary movies."

In the foyer, Wallace moved a coat off the entryway bench so he could sit down. "Y'all hungry? Ey." Wallace pulled my broken glasses from underneath him. "These yours?" He held the one good lens to my eye and I had a moment of clarity. "Can you see?"

"Yeah." Seeing our foyer, I felt all of the heat shut out of my body and a cold weight pour in.

"Y'all check the kitchen?" Wallace let his arm drop and my vision went.

"They would have heard me calling," said Nahala. "You two do what you want, I'm gonna wait in the car."

But I had to make certain. I left Wallace and Nahala and walked, a kid displaced, into the deserted rooms I'd once inhabited through a house that felt visited by the plague. I went into the living room and through the dining room where Jac-quon's high chair stood, its white tray flipped up, cereal alpha-bets glued to the bottom by old milk, but I never made it to the kitchen cuz there was a bloodstain burning the beige carpet before the linoleum.

I screamed.

"Is it wet?" Wallace whispered from somewhere behind me.

"I ain't touching it," hissed Nahala.

"You hear that?" I asked but could not turn my body.

"Sirens," Nahala murmured.

Wallace walked in front of me, squatting over the stain.

"Are they coming closer?" I asked, the siren's bullying wail like a bubble rising.

"They not for us," I heard Wallace say as the edges of my world curled/burned gray.

"Hey." Nahala pulled at me. "James."

"/"

"James!"

"/"

"James?"

"/?"

"It ain't blood," she said.

And I dropped into her arms, the living having gone out of my boy's legs.

"It's coffee," she told me as they helped me escape. "You okay, little man," Wallace said, carrying me out, "we got you— you okay."

But it wasn't me who wouldn't be okay, it was them, him, the little brother I was leaving behind.

Snake Doctors

Almost four years ago in February of 1999, my mother called to tell me that my grandfather had died. Such an announcement is not an unprecedented occurrence in the life of a thirty-two-year-old man, but what makes it remarkable is that I had not known he was alive. My grandfather, Robert Sibley, had gone to prison in 1938, leaving his wife, my grandmother, Lorene, three months pregnant with their first and only child. It had always been my understanding that he'd died in prison.

Ever since her last divorce, my mother calls me whenever she is upset. I am much more amenable to conversation than my brother, who is somewhat of a hermit in West Texas and considering jettisoning his phone. After an inquiry into my health (I am severely diabetic), she told me that she had received a letter from my grandfather's lawyer containing a strange document, which she described as a joint confession by Robert and his twin sister, Izabel. But one extraordinary observation I wish to make here, is that my great-aunt, Izabel, died in the hospital at the age of seven in 1925 from a severe bout of polio. With my mother's permission, I have reprinted the original unedited manuscript here in its entirety. I welcome readers, especially those familiar with my family's colorful history, to write in.

Saul R. Sibley, January 2003

ROBERT

This is how it went: my sister curled across the backseat of my Chevrolet, her tiny, twisted feet dangling above the floorboard. My new wife, Lorene, sitting up front, digging her body against me as I drove. When we had left Texas in the dark morning heat, my sister had been asleep, and now as the sun stewed in the Arkansas sky, she still slept.

Lorene kept saying we were lost. To the dashboard, the windshield, the birds on the telephone line. We'd only been married a few months and I believed we were in love. But when I finally gave in and pulled over, rolling down the window, an odor filled the car—just like the one Mother said came from the factory. It was how the town made its money before the hospital. Strange that a town known for its cure would smell like poison. But that's how I knew we were there, that in a mile or so we would get out of the car and smooth our best, sweat-wrinkled clothes as we walked toward the white clapboard church to see my mother's body for the last time.

That's when I heard Izabel speak. "We're close," she said, pushing her words into the foul air. And I knew my sister had been awake the whole ride, dreaming of the man in the lavender and white, the doctor who had injected his "cure" into our mother's cancerous veins.

IZABEL

After Mother's funeral, we drove to our room in the Tourist Court and I yanked off my smart shoes, taking my old pair from the suitcase. "It's too hot to go into town," Lorene said from the cot, trying to pull her dull copper bangs over bald eyebrows with fingers so fat she couldn't get her wedding ring off without soap. Pale old Lorene who had married my brother only six months ago.

"I'm not hot," I said, tying on my shoes, the right sole wedged for my short leg.

"Lord, and I'm tired too." She yawned.

"Who cares what you are," I said and my brother scowled at me from across the room with narrowed eyes. We have dark eyes. Russian eyes Mother said. Black Sunday eyes Robert called them. He pushed up his glasses, then switched on the electric fan.

"Oh my, that's better," said Lorene, posing for him, disheveled on the double cot. Touching her thin bangs over and over.

Brothers and sisters—the pastor had spoken as if before a crowd, though there was only the three of us there— *He who believes in me will live, even though he dies.* Not even a headstone saying Clementine Sibley 1894–1938 because it was not ready in time.

Brother and sisters—the pastor who had only half his damn teeth—*We commit this body to the ground.* The sermon all wrong for the lovely stranger he had come to talk about. Apple blossoms in the dirt. Pink in the white of them: the flush before good-bye. No crowd. None of the good dancers who used to drive Mother around. Only Robert, me, and old Lorene.

Brothers and sisters cried the man in lavender and white during his radio show that came on at one in the morning every night—*There is no need for radiotherapy or the disfiguring knife of the radical mastectomy.* And Mother, whose waist had become hollowed and sour, whose cancerous nipples were wont to bleed, turned up the volume and pushed her aching head to the speakers.

"You want to go into town for god knows what reason," said Lorene, pulling a stained Sears and Roebuck catalog off the nightstand. "But look at you, you're overfatigued."

"I'm fine," I said, my thumb on the scissors in my pocket.

"I read that too much sleep makes you just as tired as if you hadn't got any." She tore a page from the catalog.

Robert, my twin, held out a bottle of Coke. "Drink this. It'll wake you up."

But I turned away and went to pack my smart shoes. Mother had bought them last year. They rubbed my left heel so hard it bled. In the shoe store, the salesman's hand had disappeared up Mother's calf. They went into the back room while I waited at the counter. Ring the bell if my boss comes by, the salesman said. It takes pain to be beautiful, Mother told us.

"I'm going," Robert said, hitting the top of the bottle on the dresser. The cap flipped over on the carpet.

"That's mine," I said.

"I guess you already drank yours." He took a sip.

"No, I didn't."

He shrugged. "You can have this one."

"You already drank half of it."

He handed my Coke to Lorene.

"Thank you, honey," Lorene said, elbowing her way up to sitting to take it. "Listen," she said.

Robert turned to her. I looked out of the window over the grimy, orange kitchenette.

"We've been through just about the hardest thing, laying Mother Clementine in her grave. But she is right with Jesus and that's what matters." She set the Coke on the nightstand.

Robert nodded to please her.

"Honey," she continued, arranging her slip to hide her varicose veins, "I'm feeling poorly. You understand why, don't you? Could you get me a little hooch? Just a little won't hurt a thing."

"I guess." Robert took off his black fedora. He looked older than me, his forehead all creased, though he was only older by a minute.

"Don't forget to keep your hat on if you go out in that sun," she said.

I snatched the Coke from the nighstand and rushed out.

"Robert!" I heard Lorene whine then yell at me: "Wait!"

But I was gone, Coke spilling over the sleeve of my borrowed black dress as I limped down the gravel path.

ROBERT

It was easy to catch up with my sister and trail her through the winding blocks of stone buildings and gingerbread houses. When she stopped outside a bakery, I stopped to clean my glasses. Inside, a woman behind the window's yellow cursive was holding high a rolling pin.

"I know what you're up to," I said, watching the woman flatten the dough until it was smooth.

"Oh do you now."

"I didn't say anything because I didn't want to worry Lorene."

My sister began watching the woman behind the window too.

"The man in lavender and white," I said. That was what Mother had called the doctor because those were the only colors he wore.

Izabel shrugged. "I want to see him for myself."

"So he couldn't stop her from dying. Who but the Lord can do that?" I loosened my collar and tie.

She started walking, saying over her shoulder, "He's a quack. Somebody should put a stop to him."

I stepped in front of her outside the drugstore. "And it's going to be you?"

She said nothing, jamming her hands into the pockets of her dress.

"C'mon, let's go back, have a meal. Lorene will be wondering where we got to."

"You're not going to keep me from him." She went around me.

I yanked her back by the elbow. "I could if I wanted."

She laughed just to get at me. I slapped my hands down on both her shoulders, digging my fingers in. She sighed like the hurt was a relief.

I let go, glancing in the drugstore to see if anybody saw me. "I didn't mean to," I said.

"You never do." She stared hard at the sidewalk.

I was surprised. Usually she got nasty when I hurt her accidentally. "You can holler at him all you like, Iz, but nothing you can say will change a thing."

"Why not?"

"Because he's crazy and rich."

She rubbed her shoulders. "Rich off of people who sold everything because they thought they'd get well."

I began to rub her shoulders too. "There aren't any cures for pain," I said. "You get duped if you go looking for them."

Lorene was right, she looked tired. Her big beautiful dark eyes scraped out. "A day like today we can do what we want," she said.

I tried to distract her. "Look at that." I pointed. In the drugstore window, a gold-braided felt elephant was hanging from a lilac string. "When we were little, we had one just like that," I said. She turned to watch the elephant spin and I felt soothed like Mother was standing behind us saying, "We'll see."

"I've been meaning to tell you something," I said. I could tell that already my tone made her nervous. "Now's probably not the best time—finances being what they are—but Lorene's going to have a baby. She wanted to tell you herself, though I figured it was better if I did." Then I smiled like I thought I should.

"What do you want me to say?" she said.

"Are you happy for me?"

"You don't have money for a baby."

"We'll manage." My collar still felt too tight. I undid another button. "It's gotta rain in Panhandle someday. I'll get another job and maybe soon we could buy the house back."

"Go in and get the elephant," she said.

"I don't have enough on me. You want a doughnut?"

She shook her head. "How can you be hungry today of all days?"

"I'm thirsty too."

She got excited. "We could go drink from the creek. They built the whole town over it. It's supposed to heal. Mother said it was holy to the Indians."

"We should get back, Iz. Lorene . . ."

"I'll go to the hospital by myself," she said.

"You're crazy if you think you're going there without me."

"Come on then." She gave me a sly smile. "I'm happy for you."

We went past a post office choking on green ivy, past a hotel with a wooden cuckoo clock, and stopped at the top of a road washed green under the arch of the trees.

"This is the way," Izabel said, shifting deeper into her right hip. I gave her my arm and she leaned on me as we turned to look behind us down the slope of the street. At its bottom was the car parked in the Tourist Court, Mother in her new grave, and my unborn baby in Lorene.

IZABEL

We walked through a maze of white gazebos toward the cancer hospital, which had once been a grand hotel. At the entrance, a starched nurse pushed a wheelchaired lady across the lawn.

My brother swept off his hat before the women. "Good afternoon," he said.

"Good afternoon." They nodded.

"My name is Robert Sibley and I'd like to speak with the doctor if I could."

So polite, cautious even. I knew better and said nothing. I was busy watching the windows for a glimpse of lavender and white. A white tie. A white jacket. A lavender cravat. He thought they were the two most beautiful colors in the world. Or at least they foretold of a long life without debt.

The nurse smiled, blond and soft in white. "Do you have an appointment?"

"No, ma'am," Robert said. "My mother, Clementine died here and I'm hoping he could speak about her last days."

"You poor dear," said the lady in the wheelchair.

The nurse stroked the lady's hair like a little girl plays with her second best doll. "I'm sorry but the doctor is busy on his rounds. I will certainly tell him that you were here."

Robert was about to walk away. I put my hand on his arm. "How long will he be?" he asked.

"Oh I'm afraid the doctor won't be done until late tonight." The nurse bent over a white table and poured from a pitcher of water. She handed the woman a full glass. "Water?" she asked us.

"Did you know my mother?" I asked the nurse. "Clementine Sibley."

Under her smile, I could see the nurse getting anxious. She didn't want me talking about patients dying, that here it was all they ever did, that the only ones to walk out were the ones who had never been sick—only the hypochondriacs with their ulcerated eyes and their clean clean bodies left "cured."

"Clementine was a very charming woman. But she was too far along by the time she reached us. I only wish she hadn't waited so long to come. Though we never turn anybody away." The nurse smiled down at the woman. "Because I can't tell you how many times I've seen the hardest case leave cancer free."

I looked at the woman in the wheelchair, too weak to walk. She called us poor, but she was the fool who had likely sold every last thing to die alone in pain. "What kind of cancer do you have?" I put my hands in my pocket and felt for the scissors. "The truth is," I said, "you have to get it cut out and they don't believe in that here."

"Poor thing," the nurse said to the woman almost confidentially. "There's all kinds of grief."

Robert took me by the wrist but I kept talking. "At first you'll feel better, then you'll feel worse, and they tell you that's exactly how you're supposed to feel so that in the end you're too sick to leave."

The woman tried to wheel herself away, dropping her glass. "You let that be," the nurse said. "Let me wheel you back into the shade." She took the handles of the wheelchair, saying, "I'm sorry for your loss."

Robert dragged me across the lawn until we were behind a statue of stone horses attempting escape. I tried to pull loose but he hugged me tight, our faces so close I could see under his nose where he had cut himself shaving. In the fuss, it had started to bleed.

"See everybody's sorry," he said.

Why did he give up so easy? My twin, my brother, both of us out of the same body.

"Just let it be."

We could have found the man in lavender and white right then.

"You're not breathing—breathe."

So I breathed in Robert and the horses and a world that didn't have my mother in it.

ROBERT

We walked off the road and through the woods to the creek. The so-called healing waters. But it couldn't ever cure us.

I knew she was mad at me because I was mad at her. It was already a hard day—why'd she have to go and make it harder? We burned under every word, every turn of the head.

We stopped at the bank overlooking the creek, the water wide and deep enough to reflect the trees, the sound of it a relief. I found a patch of open grass and sat down to roll some tobacco. "Be careful," I said, "there's snakes."

"I love the water," she said, ignoring me.

I pointed at the dragonflies floating between the pines. "See, snake doctors all over the place." When I'd finished rolling a cigarette, I said, "You think I don't know about Mother."

Izabel picked up a big, mossed stick and sat down with her right leg straight. She looked like a puppet with a couple of snapped strings. "Just small town gossip," she said.

But when Mother came home late, you could smell where she'd been. "Lorene says the whole town knows." A smell like curdled milk but sweet.

"Lorene's just jealous," Izabel said, grinding the stick into the dirt.

"Of what?"

"She's already sagging."

"Shut your mouth."

"You married her not me." She was writing her name in the dirt.

"They call Mother the town whore."

Izabel threw the stick at me. It hit me in the chest, staining my white shirt. I grabbed it off the ground and she scrambled up. "Don't," she said.

It was like a hot tightness wanted out of my skin and the only way was to hit something. I swung the stick. It missed. A practice swing. I only needed to hit her once and then I'd be done. It'd be all out. Then I'd feel empty and clean and sorry. And I'd love her. I'd be flooded with love. It always came rushing right back afterward.

I whacked her in the hip and she yelped. I wouldn't have done it again if she hadn't smiled. Maybe it was nerves. Maybe spite. But she smiled.

I swung hard and hit her leg. She cried out, stumbling back, looking behind her at the creek, then quickly back up at me.

"Don't," I said, dropping the stick.

But it hadn't even hit the ground before she was making for the bank's edge. I'd never seen her move so fast. I came after her as she went sliding down the bank and into the creek, falling forward, her head going under the thick current, mud on the bottom loosening, clouding the water and swallowing her whole.

When Mother brought Izabel home from the polio ward, where for weeks she'd been sealed off in a little cell with a window like the porthole of a sunken ship, I was so much bigger than my sister that I could pick her up, and I did, carrying her from the car to the kitchen where Mother opened a jar of cherries and we stuck in our whole hands, and Mother, still a girl herself, didn't get mad but laughed at the sweet red mess. She scooped Izabel up and ran down to our pond, where she put a hand under my sister's back while she floated, saying, "Now doesn't that feel good?" And I knew it did, everything did because we had a beautiful mother we could touch.

I jumped in and found my feet could feel the bottom. I waded to her as quick as I could, going under so I could lift her up. She coughed into my shoulder as I carried her back up the incline of the muddy bank. "Are you hurt?" I asked, setting her down.

She sat with her hands covering her face. "I'm fine," she said but couldn't stop shaking.

"Dammit." I looked away while she tried to compose herself. "I dropped my cigarette. Probably set the woods on fire." I bent to slap the weeds from her wet dress.

I found the cigarette still burning and began smoking it, wandering my patch of grass. Izabel came and leaned against a tree, and as she wrung out her skirt, I saw something heavy in her pocket.

"What's that?" I pointed.

"Scissors," she said.

"Why are you carrying them?"

"They were Mother's. I brought them from home."

She stood there, squeezing the water from her dark hair and I knew I should ask something more but didn't.

I stamped out my cigarette. "I know she wasn't a whore, but those men treated her like she was."

She rubbed her hip. "Or maybe they liked her but nobody wanted to get married."

"That's Mother talking. Here." I came over and slipped off her shoes and shook the water out. "Sit down if you're hurting."

"I don't want to get my dress muddy."

"Iz, how would you have liked to go around town, running into men—damn ugly men—having them smile at you because they know and you know that they've been all over your mother?"

"Put my shoes back on," she said.

I slid them on her feet. "Let's go," I said.

Izabel rubbed the dirt off her hands. "No, not yet."

"You're tired." I didn't like the look on her face.

She hobbled over and made me sit, taking off my hat and pushing the hair from my forehead. Standing over me, she drew lines with her fingers on my scalp. "There's only one thing to do," she said.

"You keep saying the doctor took our money but she took it first. She's the one who sold the house."

Izabel's hands went still. "We have to kill the man in lavender and white," she said.

The night before Mother left for the hospital, I found her naked on her knees in the kitchen. Not a light on. Maybe she was praying. I don't know what she was doing. When I put her to bed, I could smell liquor sour on her breath. I didn't want her going to the hospital in Arkansas. I wanted her to stay in Texas and have the surgery. I sat with her until the early hours of the morning. When I got up and went into the kitchen, I found Izabel with her head down on the kitchen table, the sun creeping up her crooked waist. She turned her head. We both knew Mother was falling for another phony, the last man who would tell her whatever she wanted to hear.

IZABEL

At the Tourist Court, Lorene started me a bath, pretending to be sweet but feeling smug. Then she sat and smoked on the toilet while I sat on the edge of the bath, waiting for the hot water to cover my dirty feet.

"Nice big ole bathtub, ain't it," Lorene said. "Be good to have one like it at home." She cocked back her head and blew smoke at the ceiling. "You were gone a long time. What kept you?"

"I'm a slow walker." I began to unbutton my dress.

"What happened to your clothes?"

I said nothing looking at the mud drying on my hem.

"You're in a mood. Did you slip?" Lorene pressed her lips together and smiled. "I'll stay for a little while and make sure you don't slip again."

Our eyes met.

"Go away," I said.

She stubbed her cigarette out in the sink, took the pack from the top of the toilet, leaned back, and lit another. "C'mon honey, don't be shy."

Was my brother really in love with Lorene? When Mother

was in love, she would run a fever. She couldn't eat or sleep. She would whistle in the garden, her hands beating the dirt.

"Stay or go—I don't care."

I got up and yanked the shower curtain around the tub then went behind the curtain and finished unbuttoning my dress, pulling it over my head and dropping it on the floor. I unlocked my stiff right knee, my hands helping it to bend, and slipped under the water. When I stuck my head out from behind the curtain, I saw that Lorene was inspecting a pimple in the mirror.

"You think you know me," I said, soaping my arms, shoulder to nails. Then my waist, my womanhood, my legs, and my tiny, twisted feet.

"You know we've lived in the same town for years," Lorene said, "but your family always kept apart. That was your mother's doing. I don't want to speak ill, but that was her way of acting high and mighty, though truth be told, it didn't hide what folks knew." She waited. "Ain't you gonna say any thing at all?"

I wobbled up with a splash, the water glazing my tilted hips, the curve of my spine, my whittled short right leg, and pulled open the curtain.

Lorene looked up, staring at the red welts Robert had made with the stick.

"See," I said, "I didn't slip."

Lorene drank the gin Robert bought and fell asleep on the cot. I lay down on a blanket on the floor in Mother's old nightdress. Robert came out from the bathroom. "We'll leave in the morning," he said, setting his glasses on the nightstand. Without his glasses, he looked more like me. "Why don't you go up on the cot next to Lorene?" he said.

I turned onto my side to see his face, slipping my hand under the pillow. "Remember when we thought the world was ending? That Sunday the duster came so thick and fast, and I couldn't find you," I said.

"I was in the yard." He lay back on the cot, his hands behind his head. "It got real cold and windy. Then black. I could hear the birds going nuts, but I couldn't see a thing."

"It swallowed the sun and made us blind."

"Then I heard you calling and I crawled to the house. Where was Mother?" he whispered.

"At the doctor."

"The doctor's closed on Sunday."

I turned onto my back. "Remember we sat wrapped in that wet sheet for hours."

"Remember you saying it was like Pompeii?"

"That like them we would suffocate."

"That it was the End Days."

"This is just like then."

"But then there was a next day, and a next. We only have to wake up."

I got up, pushing on my damp shoes. "I'm going with or without you," I said.

"It was her choice to come here." He rolled over, his face turned from me. "She was going to die anyway."

"Not alone in a hospital room." I walked out the door.

Outside, the warm air wanted to be close. There was no part of me it did not find. I climbed into Robert's car, shutting the door and sinking into the seat as if it were hot sand. I watched Robert hurry from the bungalow and run to the top of the Tourist Court's drive, stopping to peer both ways down the empty road.

I pushed the car door open calling to him in a low voice. He looked frightened when he turned. The lump in his throat was mine.

On those warm midnights when we waited up for Mother, we would tell stories, sing, dance, howl—anything to fill the house. But we would never talk about the men, never mention their names or wonder where they'd gone. All my life, I loved only her and Robert, and so did not understand how you could let someone you did not love inside you.

ROBERT

I parked at the foot of the drive leading up to the hospital. Izabel got out first, stopping in front of the headlights, her face smooth like it was made of marble. I turned off the car and found her in the dark.

We went across the lawn, past the gazebos to the back entrance of the hospital. When she opened the door, light from a crystal chandelier dropped onto her hair like the moon on water. I stood a foot behind her, hatless in still wet shoes. Through the door, there was a staircase and farther down the hall, I could see the front lobby where two china dogs stood guarding a giant white stone fireplace. Izabel brought out the scissors and my face went hot, my head too light.

"Come on," she whispered.

"Wait." I tried to think of something. "Scissors?" I said.

"They're sharp."

"You should've brought a gun. Or at least a knife." I waved the gnats from my face. "Even if you stabbed him, it wouldn't kill him, it'd only make a mess."

"Not if I get him right in the neck."

"You're not tall enough," I said.

"I'll ask him to kneel down and pray with me for her."

"He'd overpower you, easy."

"I'm going," she said, and I could see that her hands were shaking. "Are you coming?"

I wished we were still on the floor of the Tourist Court, wished that we had never come, wished she could just be filled with dumb love and never feel what was not fair.

"No," I said and the door closed, leaving me standing in the dark, croaking night.

I cracked the door and watched her go toward the staircase, its walls pink with gold flowers, when the blond nurse from the afternoon appeared in the hall pushing a gurney. I opened the door wider, thinking Izabel would run back out, but instead she turned and limped up the stairs.

"You're not allowed in here," the nurse cried, going after her and dragging her back down by the arm. I stepped into the hall. Izabel swung around and without thinking—for it was just the pure clean release of the poison for which there is no cure—drove the scissors into the nurse's waist. The nurse screamed, clutching at the red eating the white of her uniform.

Izabel toppled backward, letting go of the scissors now lodged in the nurse's body. She didn't try to get up, but stayed sprawled on the last few steps, staring at the nurse where she'd collapsed on the hall floor white and sweating, her blood all over the tile.

I stepped carefully around the nurse and helped my sister up. She was so light—it was like she was not even there.

The nurse wasn't moving much but her eyes were on me like she thought I would help her.

"I need the scissors," said my sister. "They're Mother's."

"I'm not getting them," I said and my head filled again with hot air.

We stood over the nurse who was sobbing now in a blind, lost way. I thought of my mother in her last hour, alone and in enough pain to have forgotten where she was, maybe her name, us.

"She might live," said Izabel.

I drove west, leaving the nurse, Lorene, Mother, the baby— everyone but my sister, until they put her in a little cell again.

AFTERWORD

After some investigation, I located the records of the case, which found Robert Sibley guilty of manslaughter at the courthouse in Dalhart. Evidently, the nurse he stabbed died in the early hours of the morning. Of course, there was no mention of Izabel. I have gone through each of the scenes multiple times and realized that the other characters were only ever truly speaking to Robert, and that Izabel existed for him alone. Was my grandfather haunted all his life by his sister? Or did he conjure her ghost in 1938 to spur him to vengeance when their mother died of cancer at a hospital of ill-repute? Questions like these are impossible to answer and maddening to raise.

The man in lavender and white, the founder and self-appointed "doctor" running the cancer hospital in Arkansas, makes no appearance in these particular transcripts, though upon further research it seems that he does come to his own sad end: dying alone on a boat of cirrhosis of the liver, a submachine gun his only companion.

Saul R. Sibley, January 2003

The Mourners

The clocks had been stopped and she did not know if a day had yet passed only that it had been light then dark, and now the light had come again, but had it yet been a day? In this uncertain passage of time, she had not had thought. Instead a road of airless wool had unfurled wide in her head, winding monotonous through the astonishment of her loss.

Just before, when Henry had lain swamped in his own blood, his wife had heard his mother telling the new Negro cook as they stood outside the bedroom door with the dinner tray: "There is an art to dying and the boy does not have it—never mind he has been dying since first he was born." Out the bedroom window in the fermenting dark, a loose dog had again started baying. "Should I turn over a shoe, Henry?" his wife had asked, wiping her folded handkerchief across his mouth. Henry's eyes were closed, active in their closing, the collar of his nightshirt flecked red. Having been married to him fifteen years she had grown accustomed to his notseeing. Notseeing his mother's slights when first he brought her to Mississippi. Notseeing her unseemly origins. Notseeing her father's vulgar, dubious profession. Notseeing Judah's exhausted frailty betrayed by the transparency of that child's skull.

For days now his wife had heard voices speaking of her, the Yankee, so of course a Negro lover, a motherless daughter who had entrapped Henry. Whether this was spoken as she sat there in the swelter of the parlor as the townsfolk came in to view the body she could not tell, she knew only that the voices were those of women.

Her own mother had not bothered giving her a name. Perhaps predicting that she would not live past birth, it then being a time of yellow fever, or perhaps imagining that if she were to survive girlhood, she would enter into the fleshly profession, adopting a name meant to jollify men—Diamond Dolly, Baby Minnie, Big Kitty—rendering a name prior to that undertaking inconsequential. It was her father who had named her Emmeline. Emmeline, after his sister who while still a girl had fallen from a tenement window in the Lower East Side.

Emmeline stood in the stately plush oppression of the parlor and went to where her husband had been placed, propped, arranged, displayed, to where the day was finding its way into his body, choking the candles and compression of flowers.

That rot in the heat could not be her Henry. The dull gold hair she had combed and cut, the smooth emaciated body she had bathed, making certain to touch every part—the left hollow of his collarbone, the stilldamp behind his knees, the indent of his lower back—because it was said that a dead person's spirit could enter through your hands she had gripped and kneaded his fast ossifying skin, pinching his spirit into hers.

For it was through the body that they had first understood

each other. When first he saw her outside of the finishing school, he had taken her hand as if he had been waiting for her.

His dying left her in a strange muscular silence: a black halo of notsound. If ever they were to speak again it must be now through the spirit.

She closed her eyes and traced the scrolled back of the sofa to the center of the parlor, nipping her shin on a serving tray. She walked until she banged into the wall, bruising her left knee, sliding along until she felt the door. When she opened it, she opened her eyes.

No sunlight striping the hall's floral patterned wallpaper. No pallbearers coming to carry him away. Nobody to tell her if it had yet been a day and if she, Emmeline, once the wife of Henry Stovall, was free to leave his body.

><

Emmeline was not seen leaving the house except for Sundays. On the church bench, the weeping veil of black crepe could not wholly hide her, but she felt sequestered, screened. Only Judah, squirming on her lap, could slip under and touch, his fingers reminding with their hot wet that though no longer a wife, she must be a mother. The baby clutched her skirts as if trying to steer her, melting his yellow curls into folds of her heavy black serge. Kissing his hands was enough to make him smile for she was his religion.

Every night before midnight, Emmeline let herself out of the whitewashed front door and hastened down the line of cedars clotting the path, her skirts rushing over the ivy trailing down the roots as a net of branches spread above, dissecting the night sky.

Over Henry's grave, the damp silence was swallowed thick and she was nakedly awake in the stutter of birds and stars calling through the melt and sway of Spanish moss suffocating the trees.

HENRY JAMES STOVALL
1855–1889

She called but he would not come.

➤◄

Nine months passed before Emmeline received a letter from her father, Zebediah Ferris. In it, he made no mention of Henry, or of the year and a day that a widow must wait when in deep mourning. He wrote only: "I need you here."

She did not comprehend his urgency but recognized the habitual, cryptic pattern of all his attending her. When on holiday from The Select School for Young Ladies in Atlanta, she would arrive at a temporary town of picks, shovels and pans to live with him among the drinking, whoring and gambling. Either he had ignored her, or furiously concealed her in a hotel, setting Wilkie, a former buffalo hunter and his enforcer, at her door.

Emmeline could not disregard the letter. It was her father who had sent her East to the expensive school, he who made certain that her marriage to Henry Stovall, variously contested by his family, had taken place, he who had been the originator of all her good fortune and as he was fond of saying: the devil has his price.

Outside the parlor, Judah, a condensed weight on her hip, dropped his head on her breast.

"Sleepy, button? Yes, we'll do it now," she kissed and kissed him. "We'll do it quick."

Mother Stovall did not look up from her bookkeeping until Emmeline spoke saying, "Mother," and the parlor filled up with a static, continuous ire as she raised her goldgray head but not her pen asking, "Yes? What is it?"

Emmeline hesitated. "I'm afraid I've had a letter from my father."

"It's about time. I saw it delivered."

"He said that he wants—well truly he needs me to come out West. And I feel I ought." Emmeline shifted Judah onto her other hip.

"Hadn't you better not. To take a trip? Now? Why it isn't at all seemly. Write that you will come in three months."

Emmeline turned away, lingering near the piano. Judah stretched to pick the wax at the bottom of a candle perched next to the sheet music. "But how could people, Christians I mean, find fault in my traveling to see my family? Is that not a duty? Not a wise and sensible course?"

"Nonsense. The world will know it as a lack of respect for the memory of the dead. That you should have the courage to go against it—a Stovall would not contemplate it—it must be the extravagance of your age talking." Mother Stovall put down her pen. "Wasn't *Harper's* right that the sham lady will always be manifest?"

Emmeline put her chin on Judah's hair. "I have no wish to be the cause of talk, Mother." As she kissed his head, her lips felt for the thin, compact burn of a fever. She began vainly humming. He had yet to fall ill.

"Don't you take that boy if that's what you are supposing."

Emmeline opened her mouth.

"Why? Why Judah is as susceptible as ever his brothers were. Traveling for so many days on a dusty road will kill him if he isn't first slain by Indians."

"Won't my father want to see him, having never done so? He never got to meet August, or even Caleb."

"There was reason for that." Mother Stovall sniffed. "Caleb. You always had a partiality for that boy—petting him so."

Caleb had died in the time it had taken her to change her dress. He had squeezed her hand crying "Mama," and she had cradled him as she did the day he was born. She had not believed he could die.

"And should I care what he of nopast may desire? He whose scandalous vocation Henry did not care to dwell on, nor whoever your mother may have been, yet how could not I? Being a Stovall of Mississippi, how could not I?"

Mother Stovall had clung to this refrain for fifteen years, brandishing it whenever she could: a dull, starved outrage gone solid.

Reaching for a pinecone, Judah toppled a frame from the mantel. Emmeline crouched on the empty bricked hearth where Henry's rifle leaned with Caleb's fishing rod, saying, "Judah, now look—you almost broke it." It was a painting Mother Stovall had done: a small portrait of Henry, a blond boy in short pants. She laid it facedown on the mantel.

"As a man Henry did not have to dwell, but we women must. You and I must."

Judah kicked and Emmeline set him down, watching him toddle and yank on a curtain rope. "Gently. No, I'd not have him fall ill, of course not. Be gentle with it, Judah. And I am sorry if it gives some reason to talk, but I have to go. Mammy Eula can care for him while I'm away. It won't be for long. A week or two. It couldn't be for long."

The goldgray head lowered back to the bookkeeping, scratching over the household accounts. "What would you not do for that horror of a man? As if you are his dog and he has said, Come."

><

For what did her father need her, to what use could she, a mother, a new-made widow, a woman of thirty-two, be put to by a brothel-owner in a cowboy town? When the stage-coach rattled in and the ditched road bucked her one last time, the black lace went tight around her throat. But as the driver opened the door and her hands accepted his, the constriction of lace left her.

The two remaining passengers, a pregnant woman and a hazy notyoung whore, grimaced at the mud track meant to be a main street, at the slop pot stench of the tents, at the baleful eyes of purblind men. Emmeline stood in the center of the thoroughfare, drawing back her heavy crepe veil, letting in the din of burnt hard necks. How long it had been since she had known this incongruous measure of relief which now undid her as she staggered tranquil into the dusty hotel?

><

"Hell is in session, Emme. The town lost its marshal last month."

"Did he run, Pa?" she asked, sitting on a chair by his bed, her hands clasped tight in her lap. She could not get comfortable.

"Naw, he was strung up. Turns out he used to be a bandit before he turned lawman and had returned to the old ways. Made a miscalculation robbing a bank near Fort Worth and those folks came down here for justice. I myself could not help him though you might have said he was a friend." He said this while he paced the hotel room, a dirty glass of whiskey in hand.

"Oh dear. Well, I do hope they broke his neck first."

"Naw, not that rabble. He hung there like an angry chicken for nigh on two hours turning blood purple."

"Now Bart, you're exaggerating. It was half that, and it was a bank near Galveston not Fort Worth." Madame Cora, her dyed blond curls rolled tight to her head, in far finer dress than Emmeline, smiled triumphantly from above a cape of fox fur.

"Jeysus," said Wilkie from where he stood by the door twisting the stillred of his mustache. "Sure is durn good to see ya, Emme. You look right well. Glad you come help us with them Morgan boys."

"Shut your mouth, Wilkie," said her father finally sitting down on a chair on the other side of the bed, a ragged titan in a new suit.

Till then she had avoided the dirty patch covering his left eye, waiting for him, but in the tension of all in the room she now sensed an agreed deflection. "What happened to your eye, Pa?"

The new gauntness of the large, square face glared at her. He leaned over the bed, flipping the patch to show a ruined hole damp with healing. "The girls got the men a little too excited and they took to shooting out the lights. That's how some celebrate their salary."

She wondered why he bothered with the lie. "Who did it, Pa? Was it these Morgans?"

"I see you're still in mourning for Henry. But now ain't you always in black." His remaining eye which was also her eye scraped at her. "I reckon since you're dark, being a widow becomes you."

"Pa?" Her voice close on a whisper, as if they were alone. "The night before Henry died, I heard a dog."

"Howling?"

"Yes." She nodded, her eyes wide.

"Did you now?" He too came soft at speech but with an austerity she could not at that moment match.

"Yes Pa. Howling and howling. It wouldn't stop. I don't know whose dog—I don't know just whose it was. And it was odd but I remembered something Ma had said, and it is one of the few things I ever recall her saying to me, but when Flossie—do you remember Flossie?— was sick with fever, Ma said that when someone is dying you must go under the bed and turn over a shoe. Remember?" He was the only person she had told, could tell.

"And did you," he asked, "did you turn over a shoe?"

"I only remembered what Ma had said when I was in the garden with the minister and he was asking me what kind of coffin did I want. But when I went up and asked Henry—" She scratched her cheek. "No I didn't do it right away. Do you think, Pa—?"

"It hasn't been a year, has it, Emme dear," said Cora, folding and refolding her cape over powdered breasts. "What with losing two sons and then your husband, Lord, why you don't know yourself. It's a good thing you come here to be with us."

"I'll have to go back soon," Emmeline said.

"I thought you might bring the boy," said her father.

Her face burned for she was wishing she had not come at all. "Judah is too like his father and brothers." Emmeline untied her bonnet and smoothed the veil, seeing Judah when he woke in the morning, his undiluted joy upon seeing her face. Who else would ever look at her like that? "I suppose you want me as madam." She spoke now with the vigilant serenity which kept her intact.

"I didn't spend money on your fancy school for that. Besides, I got one here. Cora gabbles on but she knows her trade. I'll give her that much. You being the grand lady in the Old States is worth something. I ain't about to throw away all that damn accomplishment."

"And since I've come on," Cora said, "a trick here can earn five dollars—ten a week and you got fifty. We got a whole bunch of new girls too, did you see? Oh, they got to feeling blameful at the start but then they watch as their savings pile up! Emmeline honey, you could be an angel to your father now in his time of need."

"Shut your mouth, woman. There's a man who wants to meet you, a man I want you to marry."

"The man who shot out your eye?" Emmeline asked.

"The man who shot out my eye is dead."

><

"You do not mind if Wilkie remains, do you Mayor Gibson? It is a great comfort to my father to know that I am accompanied until I am able to hire a female companion."

"Dear madam, as you wish. Have you had trouble finding a suitable abigail?"

From across an unvarnished table in the shadowed vacuum of the hotel parlor, there was a brutish, glittering air about the fact that Mayor Gibson's coat reeked of cigar smoke and his breath was saccharine with brandy. He was a man who did not wear his weight well. The corpulent pucker under his eyes seemed to be dragging itself from the bone.

"Well sir, I did not know that I would be visiting for quite this long, and I find, without the least surprise, that there is a scarcity of respectable women in town."

"Ma'am, I myself will make inquires on your behalf."

"It is most kind in you," she said and smiled in her light, fatal way.

"Your father has told me that you have recently lost your husband to consumption."

"Yes sir." At his mentioning Henry, she began to detest him.

"Such a cross to bear when already you have said farewell to others. How long has it been?"

Her throat went dry. What was Judah doing now? Likely playing in the garden, or sleeping on Mammy Eula's lap. "Coming on eleven months."

"So recent, so recent. Why it might feel to you he were alive yesterday. It did so with my sweet wife and little girl child. Time passes differently for the bereaved, does it not? And when you wake in the morning, there are those first moments when you are innocent of knowing like Adam in Eden." He pressed a limp hand over her glove and through the black kid came a damp heat. "Your father said I would find us of a similar understanding."

This man she was supposed to marry was a fool. She felt behind her to where Wilkie stood, thumbs in the pockets of his shabby waistcoat, and was scalded by his notwatching.

"Sir, I will confide to you that the reason I have stayed is because I am dreadfully worried, dreadfully worried that I might lose my father." She heard her words as if someone else was speaking.

"I do believe, ma'am, that we will meet those that we have lost, that itself Death is but one level of our moving closer toward God."

"I would like . . . I do believe that as well. Yet I cannot help but feel my father is fortunate that the bullet which took his eye did not pierce his brain."

"In these parts, danger predominates in so many of our young men's dispositions."

"But sir, I have heard that these Morgan brothers are regular bandits, that they ride with posses and such, robbing the Mexican ranch—"

"As I myself am no Wild Bill, it has seemed best to let such beasts deal with their own. Is it hard on you there being no Methodist church in town? Is it possible you might find comfort at a small gathering I sometimes frequent? I could introduce you to our celebrated Miss Ada."

She finally felt she could withdraw her hand. "What takes place at these gatherings?"

"The assembled ask Miss Ada questions of metaphysical abstraction and she answers with what I would deem supernatural eloquence. You would find her elocution upon the subject of the deceased most enlightening."

"I suppose that I sometimes feel there is nothing noble in my grief." This may have been the one true thing she had spoken.

"There is that which assuages the mourner, the one who has yet not charted the passage to the grave and may have a vague horror upon its account. Why ma'am, if I could but show you the liberation that could be yours—but I do not seek to proselytize, only offer you the solace which I have found. If I could arrange it, Mrs. Stovall, would you care to join us?"

"I think—"

"Your father seemed to feel you might."

"—Yes. He is so often right," she smiled and Mayor Gibson smiled at her, wiping his hands on his thighs. "I could do with the solace you speak of. Though I can't help but think that I would know some measure of it if I knew my father were safe from the Morgans. You see, talk of them taking their revenge is all over town. It seems unjust when it was Shep Morgan who shot Pa, and Pa who was simply defending himself. But Shep being their kin, the Morgans shall never see reason."

"Would it ease your mind if I had a warrant put out for their arrest?"

"It would . . ." She pretended to be flustered. "No, yes it would, that would, it's true."

"Please do speak freely. Are we not friends?"

She decided to lower her eyes. "I don't wish to seem ungrateful, sir."

"You could never." Again, he pressed her hand.

Now she looked straight at him. "As long as the Morgan brothers are alive, my father is in danger."

"And as mayor, I could see that they hang?"

"My father believes it would ease my mind."

"And he being so often right?"

She need say nothing, she had won him, and was impatient for the game to end.

"Dear lady, I shall see it done."

"Thank you."

"Now that we are friends you must call me Jasper."

"Thank you, Jasper," she said.

➤◄

Emmeline tucked the letter in a drawer next to a memorial tintype of August, her first baby upturned and openmouthed in her arms. Henry had not wanted Caleb photographed saying

we had him for eight years, we will not forget him. He had a
signet ring made; the band filled with Caleb's hair.

The day of August's burial it had rained, but rain so light
she could not feel it, and still the dirt would not go soft, lending
the shovel a feverish tinny rasp that bit and bit. But the morning after Caleb died she and Henry walked the sunny fields,
their sweat and tears loose in the gold lead heat. Now she could
not clearly see Caleb's face. She who had made him—her and
Henry and God.

"You're a right good girl."

She turned from the dresser to face the balcony. She had to
close her eyes to say it. "My boy is ill." But he was with Mammy
Eula, a better nurse than herself, she knew. She hated hearing her
babies cry, the pained mewl that none of her words could soothe.
"I have to go back." She pulled her trunk onto the bed, opening it.

Wilkie folded his arms, as if to shrink his bulk. "He'll get
better. Don't you fuss yerself. Thet Miss Ada is a medium."

She needed fresh air, outside, the fresh air. "I'll tell Pa. I can
come back once Judah's well." From the balcony she could see
Mayor Gibson passing below. "Am I the only woman who isn't
a whore that Mayor Gibson has known in years?" She watched
as a drunk was thrown from a saloon by two men who stood
over him as he yelled. They took turns kicking and punching
him until he went quiet in the mud.

"An you wearing black. He likes thet."

"Mayor Gibson is a powerful man. He's gonna be governor
someday." Her father came into the room but not onto the balcony.

"It's all a humbug—spirit rappers," Wilkie spat.

"As long as Miss Ada ain't managed by P. T. Barnum she's
all right in my books," her father said.

"It ain't right," Wilkie said.

She felt impatient with Wilkie, her father, the choking weight of the air. "Judah is ill, Pa."

"There's always a spider bite or a cut or a cold. You can't keep them from the peril of the world—it's the world, Emme."

"Yes, but I have to go back. You do see, don't you?" The words were said with a narrowing restraint.

"You're gonna marry the mayor."

"Pa, I'm not trying to get your back up but must it be marriage?"

"Emme, that man there is a civilizee, he don't wanna be seen with no soiled dove. Decency and order, that's what this town is coming to."

She tried to wring the irritation from her voice. "But even if the mayor does hang the Morgans there will come more just like them."

"That's why I need this fellow in my pocket and your marriage is gonna put him there. I'm a man of business, I can't go around having my eye shot out by every hayseed that has a hankering, now can I?" He watched Mayor Gibson walk by the drunk and enter the saloon.

"I'll marry him when I come back, I promise."

"She's a beauty, ey?" Her father came behind her, clapping his hands down on her shoulders.

She flinched. "I will, Pa. But I have to be with Judah."

"When she was a kid and she'd play outside in the thoroughfare, grown men'd watch her and weep. Remember that Wilkie?"

"But what if he should be like Caleb or August? I have to—" She tried to twist away but he propelled her inside. He shoved her down into the chair in front of the dresser, keeping his hands on her shoulders.

"Her mother too. Some men'll perish over a woman. Not

me, but some. Emme wouldn't know but plenty tried to buy her mother off me. Lillie had a little of everything in her . . . German, Mexican, Ethiope . . . and in them days, Wilkie, any drop made you a slave."

"Is there affection, Pa? Is there any affection between us?"

He grabbed her by the jaw. "And my Emme was so pretty, so pretty—"

She tried to pry off his hands and get up but he wrapped both hands around her neck so she sat back down.

"So when the fellas came round, asking when she'd be ready to fuck, it was me—not Lillie, not the drunk with no head for business so soaked no man wanted to get horizontal with her—it was me who held them off, me who made Emme a lady and married her to money. Wilkie, I'll admit I never expected a man as wealthy as Henry Stovall, but I knew him for a reckless sort when I first laid eyes on him. Holding hands with Death all his life made him a gambler who wouldn't pay any heed to the objections of his family."

"Zeb," Wilkie said, his hands tentatively reaching.

Her father thumbed her throat. "But I still hadn't achieved a happy ending. For there was, you see, an impediment. What was that impediment, Wilkie? What was it? You remember?"

"Zeb, now I don't mean to argufy but Emme's a right biddable girl. Sho she's seen to it we'll see them Morgan boys hanged. There ain't no need to speak on days past."

"That's right, her mother. Because not only was Lillie a whore but a negress and that kind of union ain't legal in Mississippi, not then and not now, it being, according to law, incestuous and void. But as I knew Henry was the type to perish over a woman I said: pay me and they will never hear a whisper, those high-class Mississippi Stovalls. Because I am not the type to perish over a woman, because no matter what she is I am her father, I dosed Lillie's whiskey with enough laudanum to kill an elephant."

He let her go.

She stared at him in the mirror and then into her own eyes realizing that she already knew.

"Now Emme's a fine lady, she can afford to have sensibility, but not me and I tell you, Wilkie," her father said, his voice proud and violated, "how sharper than a serpent's tooth is it to have a thankless child."

➤◄

"Now you may join hands," said Miss Ada from where she sat in a bloom of crepe and camphor at the head of the table.

Mayor Gibson took Emmeline's left hand and an old woman retrieved her right. She ground her teeth so she wouldn't pull away and tried to watch the medium crease with effort then fall bland, passive for the so-called spirit, intoning: "We are here tonight to seek the divine illumination of our spirit guides."

Emmeline rolled her head from side to side, stretching her aching neck. And who indeed should be her spirit guide?

AUGUST THAYER STOVALL

1876–1876

5 mo. 11 d.

"So small, so sweet, so soon!"

CALEB EDMOND STOVALL

1877–1885

8 Y's 4 mo. 15 d.

"When blooming youth is snatch'd away!"

Henry James Stovall
1855–1889
In the 34 year of his age.
"Earth hath no sorrow that heaven cannot heal."

Not Judah. She was leaving tomorrow morning on the next stage. To please her father, she would marry the mayor, but first she would go home to her son. She needed to feel the weight of him, his damp head in the crook of her arm.

"We should all concentrate on our most pressing question with loving reverence," said Miss Ada.

Did she who could not believe in Heaven have a question? Emmeline crossed and uncrossed her legs, resisting the urge to kick. Did there exist a persistent, incorporeal presence hungry and blind and monotonous as hate, one neither wholly living or dead who by being neither was cursed to wander with eternal incomprehension of both? When death came did that which animated dissolve back into the earth, or was there some union of energy wherein some shape or rather in no shape she would be with them again? Or did the straining and longing and recoiling of this life beget nothing but a silence beyond notsound? Why did this frowsy woman not weighing a hundred pounds fetid with camphor insist on trumpeting her talent of conjuring demon or angel or humbug?

Heat soaked Emmeline's neck like a rash, sweat itching her scalp. She should say she was too hot but she shouldn't interrupt. Well and if it got worse she—

She was kneeling in a graveyard. The stone slab that covered the length of a coffin was cracked, shards of granite caved in. From the oak trees around her, music was playing: fiddles and brass, the clap of boots stamping, as if somewhere there were dancing.

"Emme?"

She heard a cough.

"Henry?"

He cleared his throat. "I can't see a damned thing."

She reached through the hole and through the dark, braying and sweet, she saw Henry's discolored face, a moving bruise under his eyes. "You've come back—" She crushed herself in him. "I just want to be with you," she said into his beard. "I just have to. I can't be without you. I don't want to, Henry!"

"Sweet girl," he said but she could not see his tongue move.

"If I die, will I get to be with you?" She kissed him and he tasted of sour earth. "You have come for me, haven't you?" She held his face in her hands, memorizing the ruin of eyes notblue.

He shook as if swimming up to her. "I don't want you to worry, darlin. He's with me now."

"Who? Caleb? Judah?"

She heard a noise and looked up. It was as if she were at the bottom of a well. Two faces peered down at her through a tunnel, a man and a woman whom she did not know. They seemed so urgent—shouting for her, though she did not know what they wanted, who they were, or now who she was, but that there was something of where they were which vaguely had to do with her, whoever she was. In this paralyzed musing she found herself, regardless of having made no decision, materializing into the room where they were, into the rolling furnace of a body which was hers.

"Emmeline, Emmeline" they insisted until she knew her name.

She lay in the dark on a sofa, the candles having gone out.

Mayor Gibson and Miss Ada were bent over her, fanning her, holding up smelling salts. She burst into tears. The silence, that black halo of notsound, had left her.

><

Emmeline slept into the next afternoon. It was almost sundown when she woke in a daze, everything tilted, the sun crackling like light rain through leaves. She thought she was in her bedroom in Mississippi hearing a baby cry in the next room. Standing, the blood roared oversweet in her ears. She saw the sealed letter on the dresser. She went to the nightstand, rinsing the sulfur from her mouth, and picked up her Bible, a wedding gift from Henry, as neither her mother nor her father had ever seen fit to give her one. But she set it back down between a bottle of perfume and her pincushion, placing the pipe that had been Henry's on its cover, and again washed her mouth. She could not taste clean.

On the balcony with the letter, the town went quiet and forgotten.

Leaving off her veil, she stumbled down to the thorough-fare. At the window of a dance hall, she watched a man two-stepping with a tawny whore and everything in her body went incredulous with ache and she knew herself to be that little girl standing outside her father's brothel, looking in the window at her glazed sharp mother tendering up her soft impervious breasts, manufacturing ardor for the men sore and mean with desire and her father at the glass saying No you cannot come in.

The men and the whores had turned to stare. She was beat-ing the window with her fists until she heard her left hand break. Then she ran through the streets until First Street, north until she reached the treeless graveyard. There, she found her mother's grave in the older section, buried under piles of stones the same as the bandits.

LILLIE FERRIS

1840–1874

"Sleep on now, and take your rest."

Cradling her aching hand, Emmeline knelt on the cracked dirt before her mother's wooden marker. "You were never like a mother . . . But I'm sorry," she cried, "I am. But now Judah's gone where do I go? I can't go back but I can't stay."

"M'am."

A young man's voice in the falling arrested dark.

"Do y'see this here? This is my younger brother. You might look at me and think well he musta been mighty young. He was, an my mamma charged me with his keeping but I guess I did not keep him."

She refused to turn to him—to the constant anonymous need of the world.

"I didn't even kill him like Cain did Abel. Naw, I did nothing but carry him until he died right there in my arms."

She felt him pressing the empty space behind her and itched with a violent grim frustration.

"It shoulda been me or Virgil or Jim. Christ, it's hard."

If she were to die here, if this man were to kill her now, what would be etched on her grave?

"Look at me, lady, I ain't bad-looking. Goddammit, I was accounted handsome back in Carolina."

Not dead but gone on before?

"Hey." His hand on her shoulder. "I swore I ain't gonna pay for it ever again after that."

Asleep in Jesus?

He pulled her. "I could use some comfort."

Blessed are they that mourn: for they shall be comforted.

"Ain't this is an old grave? Why you still wearing black?" The young man stood over her drinking from a bottle of rye in the stain of the abating twilight.

She was silent then said, "I'm a widow. This is my mother's grave."

His hand went down her arm. "Did you love him?"

Her mind's eye passed through as many images of Judah as it could conjure until he was a sleeping infant across her lap with his thin, perfect skin and lightly open mouth.

"Yer husband," he said, turning the diamond ring on her wedding finger. "The one yer widowed from."

"Of course."

"But you're gonna marry again?" He would not let go her hand. "I reckon you ought not."

"What then would you propose?"

"Honor the memory of the dead like I'm gonna."

"How do you do that?"

"I'm gonna murder the son of a bitch who kilt my little brother. Me, ma'am? I'm a thorough cutthroat."

"I'm thirsty," she said. "Would you have enough? Of the rye?"

"Would it be fittin?"

Her smile was bitter, brief. "You sir, have never been a delicately bred female at the mercy of her father."

He let her take the bottle and asked with anxious subjection, "Do I seem ugly to you?"

"How can I say when most of you is hiding under that beard."

He stared down at her mother's grave. "How did she pass?"

"She was a whore. How ever do they all pass?"

"Lillie Ferris. She related to Zebediah Ferris?"

"He's my father," she said and sweat parted down her back.

The young man seized her wrist and the bottle smashed at her feet. He dragged her to where SHEP MORGAN had been painted on a white post above a new grave. She was not afraid because it seemed to be happening so slowly.

"Why'd he have to shoot him?" He shook her. "It were an accident. Cause Shep—Shep he weren't the swaggering type. Not like the rest of us, you see?"

He shook her until she laughed. "Do I see?" she said.

He threw her away from him. "He was jest turned fourteen."

"A boy."

"Why'd he do it then?"

"Don't you know how men do?" she asked.

"I know how men die," he said.

"So do I," she said and began to walk away.

He went to her again, blocking her path. She stopped and her face hollowed with ache.

"I'm gonna kill your father. That offend you?" he enunciated this as if through her he could reach the ears of that man.

"Why should it? Very little is likely to offend me. I have spent a good amount of time among countless examples of intoxicated humanity."

"You think I am that?"

"I suppose you must be born astray like all other men. You've come of age in a time rife with fearmongering. But Henry always said that I could not fully know, being born a woman, and perhaps I don't, but then being I am on the outside perhaps I can see it all."

Because he too was a prisoner of the fragile flesh, because it would be a quick chaos that in its intricate burn would hold still time, because she could, she asked: "Would you lie with me?"

He seemed to try and outright laugh, sifting the voice that had spoken to him amongst all the other voices that had ever spoken. "You jest ask me to fuck? For a fact?" He was trembling, peering at the flat land, the backs of the buildings. "Out here?"

She stepped close enough to inspect the freckles across his sunburnt nose, the coarse twist of his red hair. He looked hungry, decorous, and young—far younger than she.

"Ain't you pledged to marry?"

"I've decided to take your advice." She began unbuttoning the neck of her dress.

His fingers trailed hers helplessly. "What'd I advise?"

"To honor death."

She led him to an open space between the graves. He took off his coat and made a bed in the dust, punching it soft.

"Is that comfortable?"

She laid back, pushing her head in the folds of his coat and feeling the ground's retreating heat. He looked away as she bunched up her skirts.

"Come here," she said.

He took off his hat and knelt between her legs, dogged and secret. "Do we—what's your name?"

"Emmeline," she said, unbuckling his pants and helping him to angle inside.

Above them, a hot wind dissolved into the dark.

Recognition

When I saw her instantly I felt that I had known her before. We smiled at each other across the small ballroom. The lift of her eyebrows, the look in her eyes—why else would she have smiled? She knew me as well. Yet I couldn't place her, couldn't remember a woman with red hair, and when I weaved my way to where she was standing by the crudité, she had vanished.

I took another glass of wine from a passing server, vaguely surprised she hadn't waited. Then one of the experts who had been on that afternoon's panel beckoned to me, demanding to know what I made of his ludicrous theory about the recent discovery of the bodies. I made some hackneyed excuse and slipped away. Of course, he only wanted to compare my work with his, in hopes that I felt my theories were being threatened, which would validate his feeble cogitations. If it weren't for the opportunity to tour the dig, I wouldn't even entertain sequestering myself in a roomful of small, tedious men in such a far-flung place.

On the second floor, I stood at the window of this unconvincing attempt of a hotel and looked out at the primordial red mesa with its vertical layers of white and red sandstone and the unquenchable man-made desert spreading at its feet. I went to the desk, scanning my notes from the panel, unable to contemplate even outlining my article on submerged sectarian movements. Nor could I imagine how logging the panel's pedantic minutiae would add anything substantial to my book. For a moment, I longed to be back in that wonderful period of productive isolation two years ago where I kept myself alive on dried cranberries. But inspiration would have to wait until I viewed the dig in the morning. I was, after all, the unofficial guest of honor.

I slipped off my shoes and lay on top of the duvet, musing instead about the red-haired woman. Brown freckles, green eyes, a round face, lushly pretty—none of that struck me as familiar. What I recognized was located in her expression, her smile. If only I could have heard her voice, I felt certain I would've been able to place her. I went idly through a few names, students I'd had, colleagues I'd dated, but no. I yawned. It wouldn't do to stay up obsessing over a nameless woman when I needed to be at my sharpest in the morning. I resolved to find her during tomorrow's antiquated complimentary breakfast.

As I rolled onto my side, the generator kicked off. The room went fatally dark and heat crept in. I sat bolt upright. Through the window, I fancied I could make out the dig's floodlights, rows of small tents glowing in the night. But indeed, that was impossible—it was much too far away.

It was getting hotter and the blasted windows didn't open. I peeled off my blazer and unbuttoned my shirt, feeling the breath starting to stack in my chest. I took a sip of rainwater from the glass on the bedside table and could distinguish voices in the hall, then the generator clicked into rhythm and there was a wash of cold air, light.

◑

In the morning, I woke hours before breakfast and wandered the hotel's maroon lobby wondering why it had been done in a style contemporary fifty years ago. Saturated in mauve, gold and beige, it tried to exude the confidence of a gleaming sterility, simply unattainable in this day and age. The front desk was curiously unmanned, but I managed to scare up a cup of coffee and stepped outside, walking past the landscaped cacti. A valet getting into a jeep glanced at me. Guests weren't supposed to venture beyond the drive without water or a guide. Or a gun, some said, as if the doomers still eking out an existence here were lurking, violently resentful at our curiosity. But it was the desert itself that offered hostility. Particularly, the man-made desert. Or that was my perspective on radically consumed spaces. Bibb's advocating for a return to fear, was what my detractors said. A gallingly shallow misreading of my work, but I was used to it, and what was wrong with a healthy dose of fear? If one feared the right thing, that was.

I went back in for a refill and when I returned, I came upon the red-haired woman standing alone at the edge of the drive, a conference brochure in hand. As I approached, she turned and I said, "You look familiar."

She stared at me with her rather wide eyes and precise gaze, and I was oddly reminded that some female spiders eat their mates after copulation.

"It's not a line," I told her.

Then she laughed and seemed softer, with a hint of the maternal. "You really don't remember?"

"I'm afraid I don't." I smiled. "Lee Bibb." I put out my hand.

She took it, holding rather than shaking it. "Sydney Martin. But that's my married name. We knew each other before that."

Married. For some unfathomable reason I was instantly depressed, though we had never dated, I was peculiarly sure of it.

"I'm divorced now," Sydney said as if reading my mind. "Well separated, it's almost finalized. I've kept my married name. I've had it so long. I got married very young." This last sentence took her away and I too began to picture her very young, though I could make out gray coming in at her temples.

"Did we know each other in school? I think I'd remember if I knew you at university."

"No, even before that." She smiled, quite mischievous now.

I was thoroughly mystified. Could she have been as far back as the orphanage? My time there was relatively misty, and for a smattering of months, utterly blank. Not to imply I had been mistreated, *neglected* would be a better word. However, anyone could've read the details of my experience in one of my interviews. Perhaps we'd never met. Perhaps her name wasn't even Sydney.

"I presume this is what brought you?" I gestured to the photograph of the dig on the front of her brochure.

"Isn't it what brought everybody?" she said, managing not to sound flippant, and we both looked in the direction of the dig with a kind of reverence.

"It is a rare discovery," I said. "Perfectly preserved bodies apparently."

"They knew it would happen to them," she said in a positively dreamy tone.

I glanced at her half-closed eyes and was slightly repelled. "They had warnings certainly. There'd actually been a storm the week before, not of that magnitude, but still formidable."

To start, the community had consisted of three families who wanted to live off the grid after the war: the Corbins, Wilkes, and Ashes. Together, they bought the semiarid land dirt cheap, set up tents, and began gardening and building homes, believing they'd gotten a bargain, unaware that the land, which had long been scalped and plugged with pesticides, was turning into a desert.

In the beginning, there was enough in the water table to hold a lawn, some trees, and eventually they set up solar panels to harness the sun. Apparently, it was Dale Corbin who first sought to move away from the alternative homesteader ideals they'd loosely nourished and opened up the community to moneyed families who wanted to escape but had a nostalgic longing for playgrounds, pools, and paved roads. For Corbin, it turned out that the community was less about religion or sovereignty or major collapse as it was a way to realize a suburban utopia.

After fifteen years, there were forty-seven people. In thirty-five, there were close to two hundred souls. But by then, the water they could barely afford was no longer for sale. It was a matter of time before the land dried out. Most decamped, but those who stayed evidently became more fanatical. Though to be fair, there weren't many places that would've willingly let them in. In the end, it was reported that there were roughly thirty-six people left—plus or minus a child.

"But of course," I told Sydney, "hardly anyone imagines disaster will befall them."

"I've read your article on the Corbins," she said. "Help me understand: why only write about them and not the Ashes or Wilkes?"

"The Corbins were the first to come, last to leave. Ultimately, they had the bigger arc, unlike the Ashes and Wilkes clans who were a fairly dour lot."

"I disagree. All of their contributions built the community and should be valued," she said.

"Ah, and here I thought you were a kindred spirit."

"I think I am. But you come across as obsessed with the Corbins."

It wasn't a new criticism. I'd even heard people at the conference calling me a Corbinite—such puerile designations already cropping up. "I admit I'm fascinated by the tension between those who became considerably entrepreneurial, or sort of low-level cornucopians, versus those who were Utopian survivalists with your standard back-to-the-land composting toilets—not to imply there weren't those in between."

She considered me with those bewitching green eyes. "Have you been here before?"

I wasn't sure why she asked, since the dig had only just opened. "No," I said.

"I've been coming back here for years, long before they built this hotel. Don't you think it's beautiful?" She turned to face the desert.

I didn't think it was beautiful. Nor would I have described it as such. It was too powerful for beauty.

The armored convoys pulled up and I could tell that despite their geriatrically sized sunglasses, the sordidly muscular guides were annoyed that we were standing unattended. Suddenly aware of the time, I excused myself and returned to my room to change. As I buttoned up my shirt, I mused that Sydney had never told me where we'd met, she'd managed to thoroughly evade the question.

◢◣

Chad looked nothing like I'd been imagining. For one, he was much older than he'd sounded, on the short side with large watery blue eyes. He had donned a straw hat that could have been a sombrero and seemed to be constantly gorging on a toothpick. This was the man who had discovered the dig, and if rumor were to be believed, he had opened the hotel in hopes of a tourism boom once the dig became public. Bit of a crass move, but while others believed that the community had long since fled, Chad realized that a few diehards had tried to wait out the cataclysmic dust storm and had uncovered their preserved bodies.

"I'm a big fan." He shook my hand with clammy ardor as we met outside of the largest square of the site near the remains of a shed that had once housed the community's livestock. "I've been following your work ever since you found the recording of that underground commune—that was amazing, really masterful." He led me over to the mob of academics assembled around a wheelbarrow.

In their midst, the anxious desire to view the bodies was amplified, and the scene suddenly struck me as rather ghoulish. I was gratified that Sydney was not among us, although I surmised this was because a select few had been invited, conference attendees being virtually the lowest rung.

Chad, briefly removing his sombrero to reveal a bald dome, marched us assiduously down the dirt-hewn stairs and we descended into the site, which was roughly the size of a small town square. He chummily insisted I be next to him and as we walked, pointed into the various squares identifying animal bones, battered remnants of plastic water bottles, and scattered metal pipes—relics of the community's modest plumbing.

What was in the last square was simply extraordinary: an unearthed house, its boards peeling white paint; then to its left, an empty inground pool, the blue tiles misted with sand; and finally, across what had presumably been their main street was an empty diner, its floor partially filled with drifts of sand, the occasional red stool peeking out, and the jagged edges of what was left of its windows winking in the ruthless sun. Amidst the collective approbation, I massaged my temples, feeling a bleak headache beginning behind my eyes.

Chad motioned us inside where tufts of sagebrush and shale rock had broken through a floor littered with bits of rotted ceiling and fallen beams. "The house," he told us, "was one of the earliest built, and used, we believe, as their community center. Later structures, like their houses were much more architecturally advanced. If you look at the back of the pantry door in what was their kitchen, you can see evidence of a wonderful tradition where they recorded the children's heights over the years with lead. Some of the names still remain."

Here I noted that unlike the scholars, Chad and his coterie of *guides* acted as if this were a military operation. They were visibly armed, and with the exception of Chad's sombrero, in soldierly garb.

"Is there more than what you've dug up here? Or is this the bulk of it?" I asked, feeling a tight nausea in the pit of my stomach. I wondered if it was something I ate, then remembered that I hadn't eaten this morning.

"Do you think you've found all of the bodies?" asked the paunchy sycophant who'd tried to corner me yesterday.

"Absolutely, but we think there's much more to be found,"

Chad said, unable to contain a significantly self-satisfied smile. "We've been spending most of our time preserving the bodies."

A surge of heat flared up the back of my neck. In vain, I tried to take deep cooling breaths. But felt myself starting to drift, dark edges crackling at the corners of my consciousness, then I slipped and was a boy walking alongside my bike, the chain having slipped off yet again. I could feel my child's frustration like steam from the road after a summer rain. I was wheeling my bike home along our main street, the road's black-gray scarring the gold grass. The center of town was starkly deserted, the general store closed and the sidewalks empty, though in the distance I rather thought I could hear other children playing in the community pool. As I passed the dry fountain in the town square, I was transfixed by its stone serpent coiled in the middle with an open mouth, its ominous red tongue bleached pink from the sun. I was longing for shadow, for a glass of water, for a mother's touch on my stinging knee—the most immediate of balms.

Outside of the house the grass was dead, even the poor succulents had curled in on themselves. I heard a bell tolling in the distance as I opened the front door, calling for my mother, the chilled air swallowing my child's voice. I walked through the sunlit living room and into the kitchen where I found a mug in portentous shards on the floor.

"Mom? Dad?" I wandered up the stairs but only heard the perpetually sucking sound of the air-conditioning. In my bedroom, I washed my hands in a bowl of water and dabbed the water with a finger over my cracked lips. Then downstairs, the door slammed shut and someone came panting up the stairs. Quite soon, my mother appeared in the partially open doorway, her eyes pink and swollen.

"Here you are," she said, coming in and taking my face in her sonorous hands. "I thought I told you to be home an hour ago?" Then she let me go, her mind full of something else, but she continued to speak rather automatically. "You had me worried—I was out looking for you."

"What's wrong?" I asked.

"Nothing," she said too cheerfully, wiping her nose. "We're going for that trip. Get your bag."

"I unpacked it."

"What? Why?" She seemed momentarily aghast.

"I had to use it for school."

"Pack it again. Now."

"Where's Dad?"

She suddenly shook me roughly by the shoulders. "Just do as I said." Then she was gone.

"Can I still go to Mark's birthday party?" I asked.

"Five minutes," she called back.

However, two minutes later, she was in my room in sneakers and a backpack. I'd only just located my bag and slowly unzipped it. She snatched it from me, haphazardly stuffing clothes inside. "Downstairs," she said.

Before we stepped outside, she had me crouching down with her in the foyer while she peered through the front window, then herded me down the driveway.

"I don't want to." I tried to get loose.

"Humor me," she said, staring grimly ahead.

"Lee?" Chad had a hand on my forearm. "Are you all right?"

I turned and looked at him. "I was . . . I was dreaming."

"Your eyes were open," he said.

I became aware that the entire group was staring rather blankly at me. "I've been feeling nauseated." Though I was confounded myself, something not dissimilar had happened before while I was doing field research on the collapse of a literally underground cult. I'd felt faint in one of their tunnels and the annihilating darkness invoked an otherworldly hallucination. A peril of the job.

"Okay," said Chad, glancing at one of the guides. "Let's get you somewhere you can sit down and recoup." He smiled at the group and handed me his canteen. "Hangovers and the desert definitely don't mix." Everyone gave the usual parsimonious social laugh.

One of the guides stepped forward and began leading the group through the salient features of the white house. Chad remained with me until they were out of earshot. "Look man, I don't want to unveil the bodies without you there. Like I said when we first spoke, I really dug your article on the Corbins—you nailed their mentality. I almost felt like it was a guiding voice telling me where to look."

It was seldom that I was at a loss for words, but I was floundering now. I only wanted to get out of the dig and lie down. "I wouldn't want you to change your schedule on my account. Do carry on without me. I only need to step above ground for a few minutes at most."

"Listen Lee," he paused, "can I call you Lee?"

My eyes met his massive orbs. "I prefer Bibb."

"Bibb, we can totally wait. We want you to be there, for the article. I want our debut to be something powerful."

"It's more of an essay actually, but that's irrelevant. At any rate, I'll be back shortly." I struggled to sound rational but my desire to escape was becoming unbearable.

"Sure, sure." He clapped me too forcefully on the back and gave some sort of complex hand signal to one of the guides.

Above the dig, I felt I could breathe, though in every direction I saw nothing but unending stretches of scrub and sand and this began to overpower me. Since everyone was apparently still on-site, it was reasonably unlikely that I was being observed so I sat down, not caring what damage the dust might do to my slacks. I let my chin drop to my chest and put my hands over my burning eyes. I knew I must put a stop to these spells before I garnered the undesired reputation of wilting. Yet it struck me as bizarre that I would dream (remember?) my mother and that the narrative would be one of flight. Was there indeed a time we were forced to run away? And who was Mark?

"It's overwhelming, isn't it?"

I looked up to find Sydney above me, her hair on fire in the sun. "What are you doing here?" I said.

"I told you, I've been coming here. You could call me Chad's first guide, when guides were just people to show you the way and not thugs."

"Old friends then?" I joked.

She didn't respond to this and instead looked quite steely. "Why aren't you down there? Isn't this the moment you've been waiting for? The great unveiling."

It was a rare occasion that I would willingly conduct myself in a manner I knew to be pathetic before a powerfully attractive being, but without further ado, I stuck my head between my knees and found that my deodorant had long since failed me. "Actually, I'm feeling under the weather, and honestly, I could care less about this silly article when I should be concentrating on the last chapters of my book, which isn't principally based on this community but submerged secular communities at large. I'm on a deadline after all." I kept attempting to take deeper breaths but had the impression that there was less and less room in my chest.

"Breathe out," Sydney said. "Then you can let the air in."

I exhaled and felt the tightness rippling over my face leave. "Thank you." I sighed.

"I wonder why you're here," she said.

"Sydney"—suddenly recalling my hallucination—"I had a dream of sorts. No doubt influenced by my research on this place—I really am dehydrated."

She gave a thick, irresistible laugh. "What were you doing in your dream?"

"Running away. With my mother." Something tickled my throat and I coughed.

"Some say that childhood is a dream."

"Not anyone who's lived in an orphanage." I got to my feet and dusted off my slacks. "What was strange was that there was no father in this dream."

"Do you remember where you know me from?" she asked.

I shook my head.

"Soon," she said soothingly and somehow I felt that this was precisely the case.

We walked to the bottom of the site where everyone was waiting. The feeling that I might become faint again clung to me, and I went so far as to consider holding Sydney's hand, or asking her to take my arm, lest I keel over.

"Bibb!" Chad rushed over, slowing as he recognized Sydney. "You two know each other?"

I glanced at her serene virtually noble expression. "We met this morning."

Chad did not precisely appear pleased with this admission.

I wasn't altogether certain that he wouldn't bar her way as he stood there with his arms folded, a guide looming at his side. "You can come if you want," he finally said. I decided I would skewer him in my article.

"I know," she replied.

Chad ignored this and ushered me to the front of the group outside of the diner. The moment we entered, the air changed, as if signaling some disruption in time for in front of us were roughly thirty spontaneously desiccated bodies under gauze.

One by one, Chad's team unveiled the bodies whose skin had thinned to a brown parchment clinging to bone, each face arguably distinct, and some, if not all of their features visible. As my eye traveled down the rows, I fancied that the expression of one had something of the familiar about it. I stooped over her, close enough to touch and see the places where her skull showed through. My traitorous pulse began to quicken.

As far as I was aware, Chad was watching me with interest, so I quietly backed away from the open mouths and cringing postures to where Sydney stood near the entrance, not surveying our fascinated shock but seeming stricken. I took out my notepad, pretending to write. She stared at the bodies, looking like she might fold in on herself. I looked at the floor, or more specifically, a trail of ants on the floor to avoid looking at either her or the bodies. Soon I moved toward the door, my vision trembling, smiling and waving Chad over.

"Great work here. I'm wondering how I might get back to the hotel? I've just had a spectacular idea for the article and want to get it all down." I dug my nails into my palm in a valiant effort to stay upright.

Chad's face lit up and I fled.

Back in my room, I flopped onto the bed, trying to summon that scene in the driveway with exactitude. The sun was going down, leaving the desert black and splashing the walls with a lavalike light. I was strangely unable to think of much of anything until stars filled the darkening sky like shattered glass. Chilled, I wrapped myself in the duvet and sat cocooned by the window. When I closed my eyes, I could conjure the sliver of a vision: I saw my mother and myself at the end of our street joined by another woman and a little girl. Without speaking, we children agreed that something bad was transpiring—the presence of another child only served to seal the certainty of badness.

"Did anyone see you?" my mother asked her mother.

The little girl's mother shook her head. "They've probably noticed we're not there by now."

"Nobody will come looking right away," my mother said. "It's not far. Keep walking."

The other woman looked up at the sky. "We'd better hurry."

When I looked back at our house, the sky was so dark it had put the sun out.

I jumped. A knock at the door. Through the eyehole, I spied Sydney. I threw off the duvet and quickly dressed again.

"Was your hair always red?" I asked as I let her in.

"I dye it," she said and closed the door behind her. "Why aren't you down there celebrating with everyone?"

"After beholding those bodies, revelry doesn't quite feel seemly." I moved my papers from the room's only chair.

"You feel sorry for them?" she asked.

"Their final emotion was one of terror." I turned and looked at her. "I'm decidedly haunted by the children, and perhaps their mothers, holding them in that last, frightful moment."

"But those mothers chose to stay, forced their children to stay even when they knew a deadly dust storm was coming."

"You're right, strictly speaking. Most of them knew the storm's magnitude, but they didn't *know* what that would mean. Please, have a seat."

She sat, drawing her legs underneath her and twisting her long red braid in one hand. "We have something remarkable in common," she said, folding her hands in her lap.

Despite the fact that I'd been waiting to hear these very words, I was compelled to walk to the window and pretend to look out in order to hide my expression.

"We know what it is to survive the end of the world as we know it. To be abandoned."

Somewhat composed, I turned to look at her. "Where do I know you from?"

"You already know," she said.

"The orphanage," was my pithy reply.

"Yes." The dip of her head made me think of tulips, or the stem of a tulip. Hardy yet graceful. "Let me ask you something, Lee," she said. "Why do you advocate for a return to fear?"

"A most popular misinterpretation. I discuss the value of the emotion. Similar to pain, it is telling us something."

Echoing my earlier gesture, she gazed out at the night sky. "I've always come back here. I was old enough to remember leaving here, walking out of town until we could see the canyon. I remember how frantically my mother started digging in the ground. I had no idea what the hell she was doing until I saw the steel hatch. Then we climbed down the ladder and there it was: a huge concrete bunker stuffed with supplies for the end of the world." She smiled. "And when I asked her why are we hiding here? She told me that the biggest dust storm in our history was coming, and I was not impressed. I mean, I was a kid and dust storms had been happening ever since I could remember. They were scary and dirty but that was the way things were, you know?"

I sat on the corner of the bed. "But what about your father? Did you abandon him to this potentially lethal dust storm?"

"I don't know the exact details. All I remember is that he was a Corbin and the Corbins wanted to wait it out, they forced the whole community to wait it out. So she took off with me and another mom and her kid."

I felt the oddest sensation in my limbs like an engine had turned on in my bones. "And the other child, he was a boy?"

"Yes," she said, just like I knew she would.

"And he ended up in the orphanage like you?"

"Yes." Her eyes met mine. "You have to help me."

When I closed my eyes I could see a black ocean wave of dust rolling toward me. "Yes," I said. I was that boy.

There was only one guide on duty, since everyone else was making merry at the hotel. Once I reiterated whom I was, he was relatively happy to let us in. I was, after all, nothing but a harmless scholar, pomposity my only defense.

Outside of the diner, as one might expect, I hesitated before subjecting myself to the morbid horror of the bodies. But once Sydney went in, I had to follow, keeping my gaze as well as I could away from their petrified faces, but every once in a while my eyes strayed. The half melted children were particularly disturbing. Sydney's dissent was valid: the community's bodies didn't truly merit this sort of archaeological preservation. Once Chad had ascertained how they died, then they should have been interred, but these sort of hermetic sects provoked a gruesome fascination, as well I knew.

"Did you know any of them?" I asked.

"Yes."

I broached the question as delicately as possible. "Your parents?"

She shook her head then pointed at the nearest body. "But that was my uncle, and the swimming instructor. I feel bad that I wasn't a better student. I always gave the poor guy a hard time."

"What happened to your mother? The mothers?"

"No one was supposed to open the bunker door once the dust storm started because the place would fill with sand and we'd be buried alive. I remember my mom repeating that nine or ten times. They'd just put us in sleeping bags and given us a pack of cards. It was fun—like we were on a camping trip, until we heard this banging that kept getting louder and louder. We kids begged to know what it was, but our mothers wouldn't answer, they only exchanged looks. Then the hatch flew open and I saw my father's head. At first, I thought he'd come to join us and I was happy, but pretty soon it was clear that he'd come to take us back. It was crazy—sand was whipping round the room, and outside the sky was howling. Our mothers rushed up the stairs and forced him out and when the hatch closed behind them, the bunker went dark." She paused, swallowing until her voice came back to her.

"We waited and waited for our mothers. We waited until

we couldn't breathe. When we finally dared to open the hatch, there was no sign of anyone, the town, or any living thing." She looked away from the bodies and at me.

I knew then why my childhood was so fragmented—the trauma of losing my mother, and in such a manner. To have her hands tucking me into a sleeping bag one moment and then vanishing the next. It was interesting to see how differently Sydney and I, two children of the same traumatic event, had turned out. Her reaction was to return to the site. Whereas I, by forgetting it, had sought to catalog the tragic flaw of other sects.

"It feels so true," I said.

"It is true," she said.

I was exquisitely light-headed, barely able to breathe let alone think. "What do we do now?"

"It's a space that needs to be laid to rest. The land itself needs to heal, to be away from humans."

I nodded. I'd never felt prompted to take part in anything approaching the sacred. I'd always admired the impulse, or at least been fascinated by it, but never belonged to it.

She opened her bag and showed me a hoard of lighter fluid and matches. "I'm sure we're being filmed, so we'll have to be quick, and of course, they'll know it was us, which means we'll have to hide out in the desert for a while. I have a place we can stay. But if you're going to do this with me, you know your career will be over. Think about that."

There was a profound strumming in my chest. "Perhaps I can be a sort of radical fugitive scholar," I joked helplessly.

I reached in for a bottle of lighter fluid and solemnly doused the bodies while Sydney headed for the white house. When I threw the match, the flame spread faster than thought, fracturing the bodies' delicate shells housing their bones. Momentarily blinded by the light, an unsubstantial thing thick as dream, I thought of how I loved and feared my mother's audacity.

Then I heard a flare burst in the air and Sydney rushed back in out of breath. "We better get out of here," she said. "I don't trust that guide not to shoot at us." She grabbed my hand and we ran up the stairs of the site and toward our jeep to head into the unspeakably vast desert like we had so many years before. Then I had been so afraid, but now when I heard the screech and roar of a convoy coming upon us, I felt enveloped by the purity of a true act.

Chad pulled in front of us with two of his adherents and hopped out waving a gun, his sombrero gone and his eyes more compellingly massive than I thought possible. "What have you done?" he screamed.

"Was I a Corbin?" I asked Sydney. Despite the mayhem, or because of it, I desperately needed to know.

"Calm down," she said to Chad, putting her hands up. "What's done is done."

"Or an Ashe?" I asked.

She looked over at me. "What?"

"Was I an Ashe? Quick!"

She stared at me as if frightened. "What do you mean? Lee . . . you were never here."

But the dark heat was so dreadfully familiar, especially when she tried to run, as was the suffocating silence after the bullets, from so many guns, at such close range, had ripped into her lovely face, and too my cry at the agony only a man-made death could give.

That We May Be All One Sheepefolde, or, O Saeculum Corruptissimum

Downstairs, do the floorboards creak. The servant boy bestirred from dream. The world that wast is a pernicious, noble dream. Sometime do I suspect I am its only dreamer. For all I love are gone. The world presently gray, black, cracked, brown.

Now when I wake always my body acheth: a noxious inflammation of the stomach; divers pangs gripeth under both mine arms; a disorder which produces a constriction about my breast; and am I oft visited by horrible vomitings. Verily, the reason for waking one scarce knows, for living is a prayer that hath yet to be answered. Though long have I been frail of health, I trow that in my green old age am I too disordered, my soured skin rivelled up.

"Jerome?"

Rising from my pallet, I find my jerkin bloody. Yet, it is not I who is bleeding—never is it I who hast bled. Mercifully though the blood is not dry, none stains the blanket.

"Jerome?"

I throw off my nightcap, strip, start a fire, pull a doublet over my smock, and once the water on the hearth begins to boil, drop in my jerkin, stirring and poking out the blood.

"Jerome, art thou awake?"

Lifting my dripping jerkin from the cauldron with the poker, I hang it out the window to dry whereupon I hear the boy on the steps.

"Peace!" I shout. "Go downstairs. I come."

When I reach the bottom of the winding stair, I see that near the ware-bench, the boy is stacking books and eating a crust. He casts upon me blue eyes, free from wrangle.

"Good morrow," saith he. "Art thou hungry?"

After the fire at St. Paul's Cathedral, I moved the book-store hither. Twas not long after that when the city met with plague, and this orphan boy, then a beggarly pickthank, began haunting my pages, though he knew not how to read. It is to me an irony that I should now sell that for which men have burned.

"I fear I have no appetite this morning," I saith.

I guide him by the shoulder, walking him past the great Chaucer, *The Falls of Princes* by Lydgate, *The Passetyme of Pleasure*, the *Gesta Regum Anglorum* and *Historia Brittonum*, shelves of Italianates: Petrarch and Boccaccio, the workes of our righteous Pagans: Quintilian, Aristotle, Pliny, Plato, the epistles of Tulle . . . and take down *The Flour of Curtesye*.

"Time," quoth I, handing him the volume, "to become a lowly copyist."

At this the boy smiles. How ready he is. Never does he lament the want of a printing press and thus revile the work of transcribing.

"Shall not I first clean the upstairs?" he asks.

"Nay, I wot it does not need it and is in proper order from thy previous good services."

Upstairs, I sit heavy on my pallet and find blood creased between my fingers, dried at the hilt of my knife. Jerome he called, yet was my name once Uthred. And like the boy, was this old badger an orphan. If I could again fast knit my life to God—by God I would. For there be some mornings when I wake to bells that no longer ring, and I am returned to the days of my novitiate in the Year of Our Lord 1536 when I wast a black monk in Marston Abbey.

I did not know how I had come to be at Marston Abbey. I knew only that as a small lad I had been given unto the brothers who had taught me grammar, rhetoric, logic, liturgy, and to love God; a love which wast then as necessary and natural as breath. When tilling the fields, when collecting honey, when copying manuscripts sacred and profane, God wast with me. In this quietude did I glory.

Yet long had my lack of origins troubled me, and twas the day after our St. Swithin's Day feast when I came upon the Abbott in the Lady's Chapel, and mayhap made bold by the summer's heat, did I solicit him upon this great matter.

"Abbott," said I, "may I ask thee for counsel?"

He was sitting in a deep study under the chancel where sinners were painted falling into Hell. Around his tonsure, his hair grew grey with white and this same hair sprouted thick over his fingers. He stirred from his abstraction and did see me. "How now son Jerome?"

"Abbott, am I right thankful to offer up my service to the

abbey, but is it not fitting that I know Uthred before I become Jerome?"

"What meanest thou?"

"I know not what wast my family. If it be their wish that I become a man of God—or even which of them brought me to the abbey when I wast a child. Wast my mother? My father?"

He patted the wooden pew. "Thy mother. Dost thou not remember?"

"Nay, though now my mind conjures images to accompany the story. What was she?"

"Wherefore dost thou inquirest with so stern a brow?"

At his sudden raillery, I could not but produce a smile. "In faith, Abbott, I trow not why I should when so seldom have I meditated upon my birth."

"But now someone hast spoken words which leads thee to believe that thou hast something of which to be ashamed?"

I lowered my head in assent for too well he saw into my heart.

"Thy mother was a yeoman's daughter who had alas come in the way of a bumptious man who did not take care of her innocence and youth."

"A fallen woman?"

"We all are fallen from grace, Jerome. All of us banished from the Garden. Judge not those in need of thy compassion. She did not have the means to keep thee, nor the wish to bring ignominy on her family."

I sat full heavy with this then asked, "What county wast she of?"

"Methinketh from the east, Middlesex."

"Had she kinsfolk in our village? Is't possible she still visits? Does she know that I am here as a novice?"

The Abbott gazed into the stained glass of Our Mother. "Thy mother is no longer among the living. She did take her life after thy birth. Her spirit sank and she could not abide the sin."

Twas the loss of a thing I had never thought to imagine I had. Yet would this be a trifle against the loss which would follow the feast day of Saint Luke the Evangelist, as the leaves and the cold mists fell.

It were a morning as many a morning. I knelt on the cold stones in the new day's blue light and prayed. When I heard the bells of Matins, I slipped on my sandals, put up my hood, and rustling from my cell, went through the dormitory across the yard towards the chapel. There by God's strange glory saw I a man in a fur-trimmed jerkin, walking the arched tunnel which lined the square of the courtyard with the Subprior, followed by ten men dressed in fine livery. The man was tall with hair brownish-black. His boyhood looks could be guessed at by what remained in his face. Like the fog which had settled, I pressed my body to the walls, and none did spy me as they passed through the cloister. Much startled, I hurried onto the chapel, dipping my fingers in the holy water, taking my place at the end of the row with the other novices, waiting for the ringing bells, hastening footsteps, doors closing, to pass on unto silence.

Afterwards, I joined the other novices and met our novice master who must needs shew us how to arrange our habits, hold our hands and head, to walk with modest solemnity. None knew who the man in a fur-trimmed jerkin could be, though some had seen him enter the Abbott's parlour. That day were we to practice verse in order to have fluency whence professing God's Truth, but this was interrupted when we were told that a

Royal Commissioner, carrying a list of Instructions and set of Injunctions, had come to visit with each of us.

"Thou art the last to be summoned to stand before the Royal Commissioner," quoth the Subprior, a man of drooping eye and thick tongue, his tanned arms resting on the taut of his belly. Unlike the Abbott, all about him was pageant.

"What doth he ask of us, Brother?" I said meekly, though was I chafed by this allusion to my being not from a family of nobility or fortune.

"He is here to apply the law of God through the King. He shall have ye swear to the King's Supremacy over our church and to no longer defend the power of the pope, now Bishop of Rome."

I had heard rumor of some such thing, but hadst not believed it possible till now. "How should I answer?"

"Thou wilt do whatever is necessary for our abbey to please Master Cromwell," quoth he, churlish. "Thou wilt not obstinately stand from the Crown."

The Royal Commissioner gave a start when shyly did I enter. Behind him hung a tapestry of our Savior sitting on a Rainbow, His woundful eyes gilt with the grace of sacrifice.

"I am John Haskewell," quoth he in a voice melodious rough. "Ye be Brother Jerome?"

"Ay sir," quoth I, curious.

"And from what town comes thy family?" He examined my person with a discomfortable arrogance, then proceeded to pour himself wine.

"I know not, sir. I am an orphan. The Lord, who never forsakes, did take me up."

"Better fare than the workhouse, ey? And how many years art thou?"

"Nineteen, sir."

John Haskewell sipped from the Abbot's gold plate cup in a manner indifferent. "What dost thou copy now?"

"*Confessio Amantis* by John Gower."

He looked into the wine, reciting, "'A book between the twaie,/Somewhat of lust, somewhat of lore'?"

I flushed. "Yes, sir. Thou art familiar?"

"I?" He refilled the cup. "I got no further than 'The Book of Constance.' I verily believe thou art to be commended to journey on, Brother. Sit." He indicated a stool.

He walked up to a tapestry figured in silver and fondled the cloth. "Dear Brother Jerome, I shall not tarry: I have heard report of laxity in this abbey."

"Nay," quoth I, vexed, "I assure you, sir, tis a false report."

"Could it be that thou doth not believe a fellow monk speaks true? Would thee"—he turned back to me—"so famed within these walls for thy honesty, mark thy brother out as a liar? I profess it would displease me heartily to discover this man guilty of perjury. I so detest having to decide if a just punishment be a pillory or a hanging."

Was I clean amazed. It was many moments before I could declare any thought by mouth. "Sir, in faith, I have not known any of my brothers to ever utter an untruth."

He set down his cup, stretched his arms, then flung himself down onto the Abbot's high-backed oak chair. "I am glad to hear thee confirm his innocency, Brother." He yawned. "Howbeit, it is a great shame that your Abbott allows some monks here to be so merry drunk after Compline that they snore through the Night Office, is it not?"

"Certainly sir, have I never witnessed such acts."

"Nay? Yet thou didst tell me that none of thy brethren lie."

And thence, his frivolous aspect began to recede and his thievish eyes lit gravely upon me. "But for all that, Brother, dost thou believe Abbott Wendover art a good man?"

"The best of men. I wot of no heart more kind-conceived than the Abbott's."

"Yet he is friends with men of perverse minds, servile usurpers many of them, and thus in time may his mind be flattered into corruption. Yet thou, the chiefest bud of Marston Abbey, could guard him against such heretics."

"I am naught but a novice."

He sat up, leaning forward. "I would argue that thee art favored above others. Aye Jerome, this day have I heard it said thou art the Abbott's best loved. Why is that so? Is't thy pretty mouth?"

I looked at my sandals, vainly suppressing my complexion.

"Sweet modesty." He stood. "If thou shalt keep me abreast of the Abbott's conduct, I will write unto Master Cromwell that the Abbott is innocent. In this way we shall safeguard him and warn him of any maligners."

"Sir, it would be against my vow of obedience."

"Know ye what is writ here?" John Haskewell pointed to his letter book open on the table. "It saith that thou shalt receive no women in the abbey, not even lay servants. That none including the Abbott must leave the grounds. And that all monks under four and twenty should be dismissed. Yes, Jerome of no county and no family, ye are reckoned to be but nineteen. And where wouldst thou go? What stranger should take thee in? I verily trow that thou wilt meet me and tell me of the Abbott's doings, wilt thou not?"

I swallowed, perplexed. "Mayhap I—"

"Good lad. It is said thou art a scholar. Thou couldst be

studying true knowledge at The Schools. Fore God, what dost thou learn in this place?"

"To love and be loved by God. To love all men through God. To love as God loves."

John Haskewell's expression was soft amused. "Thine heart has no hesitation. Even if thy path is awry." He placed a hand on my head. "Kneel."

I slipped from the stool and knelt.

"Do you swear to renounce Rome, to acknowledge and confess it lawful that his Highness should be Supreme Head of the Church of England?"

My mouth obeyed.

"Ye will see no women. Ye will not leave the abbey. Though thou art nineteen, will I petition Master Cromwell to see thee spared and thus not made to leave. This service have I done for no man."

"Sir." I rose and bowed, sicklied by this sudden alliance. "Am I not unthankful."

The boy has ague. I drag my pallet closer to the fire, pour him a cup of meade, and bid him drink.

"Jerome, have I not got currants and barberries for the roasted conies," he frets.

"Marry, then shall I go to the market and get them," saith I.

"What if a customer come?"

"And pray why are ye such a woeful spirit?"

"Thou art woeful also, Jerome."

Very heavy am I following his gaze. He looks to my jerkin stirring in the window. Faith, though the blood is washed away, I cannot lightly forget. "I wish only thou wast well."

"Did thou stain it?" he asks.

"I pray thou take thy rest now." Ought I let him slumber? What if he should not wake?

Downstairs, I begin to copy *Confessio Amantis*.

Thrice John Haskewell summoned me to meet him in secret. That final night, I waited, standing under the wrathful flutter of the willow tree I loved during the day, cudgeling my mind for some such prattle to deliver which would hint at no vice— though well I knew that once in his presence, it was hard to dissemble.

As soon as he swung down from his horse, he called, "Have ye heard any lewd communication from the other monks?"

In the dark, I could not spy the familiar dissipation under his eyes, and as he neared, the shadows made his complexion smooth, adding the charm of youth to his looks.

"Nay, John."

He tied his horse to a tree. "I wot right well that the young oft find it hard to denounce the old believing they be worthy of pity."

I covered a yawn. "My brothers are men of God. To me they have talked of naught improper. Therefore, again can I not confirm thy tedious suspicion."

He had a laugh that was profuse with a music absent elsewhere in his disposition.

"And thou, Jerome?" A wet wind scattered through the

branches, discharging a decay of leaves. "Thou art young"—he walked toward me, no longer merry—"and must have longing for fleshly delights."

But did I long only for these perilous nights.

"It is not unnatural," he continued, goatish. "Not that thee have acted upon thy desires, I accuse thee not of that, but we all have our secret sins."

"It is true I am not free from sin," said I, "but none of them be secret."

He drew too close. "Thou hungerest to lie with a woman, touching the privy parts of her body, using her as a man doth his wife."

I stepped back. "Nor am I a stranger to curiosity, nor divorced from my body but delight in its workings."

He stepped with me and I could smell the wine. "Then art thou more inclined toward buggery, surrounded as thee are by these pedants. Do ye wish to play the woman with a man's cock? Do the servant boys tempt thee?"

Disgusted, I made to leave. "I need not suffer these carnal-minded accusations."

He appeared in my path. Though I was the taller was he of far greater girth. He put a hand on my shoulder as if measuring its width. "It is unkind in me to tease thee. Wisdom, thou knowest, so seldom accompanies age."

"I am tired. What is it thou desireth to know?"

"What letter did the Abbott read on the Memorial of Francis of Assisi?"

I allowed my puzzlement to show. "The letter by the Bishop of Rome?"

"It is true then. The Abbott remains loyal to the old church."

"No, the Abbott is a true servant to the King. On what charge could thee accuse him?"

"Did thou not sayeth, Brother, that thou wast troubled by a ceremony that the Abbot held exalting the Bishop of Rome? The charge is treason."

"Thou dost mangle my words!"

"My poor child." He smiled. "Have ye not bethought that there are those within these walls who are dissatisfied with the Abbott?"

Never had I the occasion to consider. "Then wherefore have need of me, if there are these others?"

"The King has no wish to see his abbots dead. And I wot the Abbott is a kindly man for all his papish folly. Thou couldst save him from a traitor's death. Tell me that he has frequented taverns or mayhap dallied in a maiden's lap, and instead of the rope, he will be deemed unfit to have charge of the abbey."

I shook my head.

"Then will he die." He shrugged away, sourish. "Fear not, when the abbey falls, I will see thee rewarded."

"My vows of chastity, obedience and poverty are my reward—I seek no more than that."

He laughed. "Without these walls thou wilt be broken ere thee hast lived an hour. Think how simple it was for a stranger to gain thy trust—to become intimate with thee?"

"But thou art not a stranger. And I know thou wouldst not see an unjust murder done. For thou knowest he is as a father to me—John!" I took him by the shoulder, directing to me his scent, his gaze, the very pith of him which was to remain to me unknown.

Mine eyes met his and I felt my spirit overcome by his practiced malaise.

"Verily," I choked, letting go, "I have known that thou wert mine enemy."

"Yet didst thou wish to love as God loves, loving even thine enemy," he mocked, then became intent, "Jerome, would thou not desire to save thy father's life?"

I stared at my tormentor in new confusion.

"Ye must know him for thy father, but it cannot be proved unless thee admit thou art his bastard. You fool, why dost thee think thou art favored?"

I pulled away and began to run. He knocked me down and when I caught back my breath, I found him kneeling at my side.

"Dost thou know who told me of the pope's letter? The Subprior." He smiled. "How easily you are surprised, little monk. Worry not, he too wilt suffer the traitor's reward. Unless thou wouldst say that thy father hast sinned. Even to say that he hast gone hawking—"

The brush had scraped my hands and feet bloody. I stood, grieved but fixed. "I should trust thee, a servant of Cromwell, that he is my father? Thou may knowest me and aread my frailty. Yea, my heart may be transparent and easy to guile—marry, to thee it is nothing but a child's toy. But thou knowest not the purity of the Abbott."

"Verily I see that thou art a proud child and thy pride wilt not permit thee to see his life spared."

I brushed the mud from my robe. "I trust in God's merciful goodness that nothing will hap to him."

The Royal Commissioners ransacked the Abbot's rooms in the morning, searching through his papers for evidence of treason against the King. After Lauds, I was about to wander back to my cell, when I was summoned to meet the Abbott in the Lady's Chapel. Though well I knew I would not find consolation in solitude, I fretted he had discovered my disloyalty.

"My son," he quoth then fell silent.

I prostrated myself before him, then sat by his side. Immediately, his accustomed bulk was of comfort.

"Abbott, I pray thou wilt submit unto John Haskewell and resign thy place."

"And what should become of ye, aged and young, were I to do so? I must away to be examined by Cromwell and Parliament, and I trust to God that I can see our abbey spared from suppression yet again."

"Abbott, prithee let me accompany thee to see Master Cromwell."

"Nay my son, the Prior and the Subprior already go."

"Abbott, I beseech thee to surrender. I know not what John Haskewell will do to thee."

"I may suffer worldly harm, but shall I suffer far less in the hereafter."

I was confounded by his sweet resolution and bowed mine head. "Yes, Abbott. Always am I helped forward by thine example."

"I beg thee not to worry, child, by God's grace shall I be wonderfully delivered. And thee must to Oxford. It is for this I have called thee."

"Oxford? No, by this light, I will stay here until thou returnest."

"Jerome, because thou hast shown thyself to be a scholar of

worth, wilt thou study at Gloucester College. This day shalt thou go."

"I had thought it was decided we had best wait till next year?"

"It hast been made possible. I trust thy wit and discretion on this matter."

I put up mine hood.

"Yes, my son?"

"My father . . ." I kept mine eyes low. "Thou saith he wast a bumptious man?"

"Oh, a waggish, vainglorious fellow."

"What did he—did he know of me?"

"He did not know of thee until long after thy birth. But when he learned of thy mother's death did he repent his former life and take orders."

"He is a monk?"

"O aye, he is an abbot."

"Oh let me come! I will tell such lies the ears of heaven will bleed but thou shalt be spared!"

He smiled but did not look upon me. "Thou must to Oxford. This is my wish."

My eyes watered sharp. "But what shall I do without thee?"

His hand took up mine. This was the hand that had first lifted me from my heart's poverty. "Suffer we, my son?"

"Yes," I said, "we suffer much."

"I trust we never suffer alone, and in that lies our salvation, in that lies the heart of God."

Men seized the Abbott, taking him to where their saddlebags were stuffed with our jewels and gold plate. John Haskewell was the last to mount, shouting: "Ye are no longer monks. Your servants are dismissed. Marston Abbey is now the property of the King." Never did he look in my direction.

Before nightfall, the townsfolk, divers of whom we brothers had tended when sick, fed when hungry, counseled when vexed, descended on the monastery, stripping the roof and pillaging relics, taking books with which to wipe their arses. I gathered what volumes I could and straightaway rode to Oxford. I wept to abandon such dear familiarity.

The boy has a fever and begs me not to give him burnt dung with honey. I tell him next he will bid me put a turnip up his nose. I say if he is good I will get him a hot codling.

By my troth, I thought I had grown weary of meddling with this world for whose wickedness there is no remedy, but now by this blood-guilt am I more than lost, now am I damned. And here do I dally in needless contemplation when I shouldst be making haste to the market to buy lavender, sage, marjoram, rose and rue to make a mixture for the boy's head. And a baked apple and those berries . . . But for what? Belike he shalt not live beyond this night, and perchance he should, am I no guide for the innocent. It is merciful to let him die, and ease his suffering.

I approach the pallet where he is sleeping, his cheek rose with heat, and think how easy t'would be to grant him everlasting sleep.

When I had word that the Abbott was being taken back to Marston, I made haste to return. It had felt unnatural to study in a walled garden of bluebells and wander the verdant hedges of Oxford with such sorrow pressing in.

I knew not then that the Abbot had had a brief trial, heard not before his peers in Parliament, but by a jury of Cromwell's false friends who had found him guilty of treason.

As I rode up, the deserted abbey was first reflected in the pond. Our roof had gone. I walked about the ruins, then saw on the hill next to The Tower, a hastily erected gallows where three ropes hung. There stood I in my dread.

Shaking sick, I prayed in what was left of the nave. Twas almost dark when I walked mine horse under the abbey gate, and there I did see where they had piked the Abbot's head.

So cumbrous was mine horror upon the gore that wast my father's face, twas the full desolation of mine heart. It was then that God left me.

Yesterday I was upstairs when I heard the boy welcome a customer. As I came down the winding stair, saw I a man bent over the boy whose countenance recalled to me John Haskewell. I stepped back into the shadow of the stair and listened to him cajole the boy, then inquire for a copy of *Confessio Amantis*. Doubtless it was he. It couldst not have been another. Always will I know that unsparing voice. When he left, I flew down, and bid the boy to close the shop.

"I must go out this night," said I.

"Can I come with you?" he asked.

"Nay, thou shalt eat thy supper and off to bed."

The boy was angry and in a manner peeved began to rekindle the fire, making more dirt than flame.

I followed John Haskewell until he stopped outside a tavern. I stayed out of the light then laggardly went in after him.

Most of the Royal Commissioners of the Suppression hadst sith been rewarded, granted lands, knighted excepting Cromwell who was beheaded by King Henry for marrying him unto the unhandsome Queen Anne. For near on thirty years, I heard nothing of John Haskewell but that some vitriol launched by him against the King's favorite had him turned off in disgrace.

Time had ravaged him. He had sith grown stout and pilgarlic, though now hadst he a thick beard. A singlewoman accosted him but he was too whittled for a dalliance and kept at the ale, jesting with any buffoon who wouldst harken. In a dark corner, recalling the treasuring safety of the abbey, those hours given over to abundant study, I drank myself merry.

When finally he left the tavern, I was fast upon him. Without thought, I, once Brother Jerome of Marston Abbey, resolved to do a murder. As he walked down a darkened alley, I struck the old knave until he staggered and fell.

"Devil take thee!" he swore. "What dost thou want of me?"

I kicked him until I could no longer.

"Look at me," I said and knelt in the muck, roasting in my scorn, pulling his face to mine. "Dost thou know me thou villainous toad?" I smashed his face into the ground.

"Sir," he tried blindly to crawl away, "whatere harm thee thinkst I have done I swear I have not!"

"Likely there is much blood on your conscience." I kicked him again and he fell flat. "But this night do I avenge my father's murder."

He cursed foully, then seemed to swoon.

I tried to shake him awake. "Do you remember Brother Jerome?"

"Who is't," he slurred awake, "who is't thou thinkst I murdered? Tell me a name . . ."

"Thou art to blame for the death of Abbot Wendover." I put my knife to his throat.

He began to sob and cough up blood. "Nay, have mercy upon me, sir." His weeping marked through the filth down his pitted face. "O God, after thy great goodness . . ."

The knife went from mine hand. As he prayed, I could not do it. Yet too late was it for mercy.

"Get to thy feet, swine." I tried to raise him up but he could not stand.

"Brother . . ." He lolled at my feet.

"Get ye home. Get up!"

His eyes slung back his head. "Dost thou know me?"

I knelt again. "I am Jerome. Thou art John—art thou not?"

He began to still. "Long I to go to God," he muttered, his eyes searching backward into the darkness of his skull.

I drew his head onto my lap. On his forehead, I marked a cross with my thumb, and prayed: "Through this holy anointing, may the Lord in his love and mercy help thee with the grace of the Holy Spirit. . . . May the Lord who frees thou from sin save thee and raise thee up. Through this holy anointing, may the Lord pardon thee what sins thou hast committed . . ."

And there on my knees did he die.

⟨⟩

Night has come and the baked apple with which I did seek to beguile the boy has grown cold. All around his head is a halo of damp. He hath caught so bad a fever he is almost dead.

"Jerome? Thirsty."

"Here." I kneel next to my pallet, lifting a cup of tea to his lips.

"Do not go."

"Pick up thy spirits. I will stay by thee."

"Jesu, am I weary."

"Ay"—I put a cool cloth over his forehead—"we are weary with our burthen."

Mayhap this boy is not for the world of men and well I know I am not worthy to guide him. Yet sweet Lord, take him not. I will not promise Thee that I can again conjure the pure faith of my youth—forgive me that at least—but let me find a way near Thee.

Make me a clean heart. Renew a right spirit within me. Cast me not away from thy presence, and take not thine holy Spirit from me. O God, in the most corrupt of centuries, hear my prayer.

The latin phrase "O saeculum corruptissimum" or "the most corrupt of centuries" comes from a letter by a sixteenth-century monk Robert Joseph and is cited in *The Division of Christendom: Christianity in the Sixteenth Century* by Hans Joachim Hillerbrand.

ETERNAL THANKS

To Denise Shannon whose luminous patience, generosity, and literary divination is unparalleled.

To Megan Lynch whose brilliance and magical literary zeal made it happen, Eleanor Kriseman, and everyone at Ecco whose incredible support brought the book into the physical world.

To Arthur Flowers, George Saunders, and Dana Spiotta, three brilliant points of light who led the way.

To the Fabulous Five: Rachel Abelson, Mildred Barya, Martin De Leon, Rebecca Fishow, and Dave Nutt whose incisive feedback and fantastic work goaded/inspired me.

To the Syracuse University Creative Writing Program for the space and time to read, to write, to be an artist.

To Carmen Amaya, my prophet and earliest reader.

To Paul Cody who was the first to go to the mat.

To Anais Koivisto, my moral center and artistic high tide.

To Linda Longo, my fairy godmother.

To Ben Marcus who plucked me out of obscurity.

To Stephen Squibb who fed me whiskey and always made me feel it was gonna happen.

To Jessie Torrisi who let me slip stories under her door.

To Baron Vaughn, my brother and best friend.

To Ryan Senser and Team 383 who were my haven.

To Leo Allen who introduced me to the mysterious workings of the S.S.S.C.

To Melissa Cleary Pearson and Vineeta Shingal whose great hearts made a small, crucial donation.

To the Colgate Writers Conference who told me I was a writer.

To Andrew Milward, Steven Barthleme and the Center for Writers at the University of Southern Mississippi; Charlie Baxter and the Breadloaf Writers Conference.

To *The American Reader*, Granta.com, *The O. Henry Prize Stories, The Cupboard, Fence*, and Bryan Hurt.

To my family who loved and made me.

To Julian Isaiah whose imminent arrival forced me to finish the book.

Last and Most to Christopher Brunt ". . . when I touch you / in each of the places we meet / in all of the lives we are, it's with hands that are dying / and resurrected." ~ Bob Hicok